Rebecca's Quilt

Fran Smith

PublishAmerica
Baltimore

First printing

ISBN: 1-4137-3968-7
PUBLISHED BY PUBLISHAMERICA, LLLP
www.publishamerica.com
Baltimore

Printed in the United States of America

I would like to acknowledge and thank the following people. Without their help, *Rebecca's Quilt* might have remained a figment of my imagination:

My mother, who encouraged me in my love of writing. My husband, who knows more than I about computers and doesn't complain when dinner's late. My stepson, Ken who knows more about computers than my husband. Susan Stanovich, Library Director at the Uxbridge Free Public Library who gifted me with a wonderful book rich in the history of Uxbridge. Anne Dansker who was kind enough to read this in the rough, and tell me when things didn't sound right; and the following people for their encouragement: my daughter Marguerite Broyhill, my cousin Phyllis Bratt, and my close friend, Maria Perry. A special thanks to a very special friend who will never see *Rebecca's Quilt* in print, Sandy Kaminsky. There's no way I can thank Barbara Bixon, sometimes known as BB Carter, who spent hours with me, encouraging, helping, then helping some more.

With people like this, how can I not sit down and write!

Chapter One

Katie had to do it now, before her mother and sisters arrived. She hesitated; in July the attic was hot, but it was now or wait until they left. She couldn't stand it, she had to see what was in the old trunk.

As she stood at the bottom of the attic stairs hairy dust balls danced down the steps toward her. She reached up and flicked on the sixty watt bulb at the head of the stairs. The light was weak, making it impossible to read the names of the magazines piled on the steps. Dusty floral vases, home to generations of tiny spiders, were scattered among the journals.

The air smelled stale. Dead.

Her grandmother's funeral was two days away. A lump the size of her fist filled her throat and tears started down her cheeks. She leaned against the bare lath wall and stared at the eighty-year collection of "things too precious to throw away." Why couldn't her grandmother have gotten rid of something just once, she wondered. Katie could hear her saying, "you never know when you might need it, Katie" and she smiled to herself

If the farm wasn't sold by September, her mother and sisters would have to come. Not that they'd like the idea, but this time, just for once, she was going to say "no" and mean it. She couldn't stay all summer, she had bills to pay, too. Teachers didn't make a lot of money.

Cheese's orange-striped periscope tail scanned the attic horizon. Maybe she'd find an old toy or a forgotten ball. The attic was cat heaven. Endless boxes, trunks, and paper bags, all waiting for her inspection.

Gram named all her orange cats Cheese, except for Brie who was cream colored. A wave of anguish flooded over Katie as memories of holidays, summers and rainy days spent at Grandma's caused her to fight back the tears.

Cheese made no pretense at being a mouser and swatted a bubble gum wrapper behind an old oak dresser. Kate laughed aloud, wondering where the wrapper came from. An unlikely picture came to mind of her grandmother with a wad of gum stuffed in one cheek.

Cheese sniffed inside a brown grocery bag stuffed with bank statements, canceled checks, receipts, and advertisements dating back to 1932, forty-one years ago. Cupcake tins, bread pans, cookie sheets, all sorts of baking implements spilled across the floor in front of two treadle sewing machines. Fishing poles languished against the chimney. Cheese sniffed the upside down Flexible Flyer, its rusty runners as lifeless as the dead flies on the window sill.

Her throat constricted again and for a moment she panicked. Fourth of July, Christmas, Birthdays and Thanksgiving memories hovered in every corner...things that could never be again.

Dust motes plodded through the heat. Kate played the flashlight across the room, stopping at the humpbacked chest under the eaves, almost hidden behind the chimney. Katie had spent years pulling and banging on that lock, but it never budged. She jumped and turned. She would have sworn she'd heard her mother say, "Stay away from that old trunk, it's got nothing but old letters in it."

She fingered the key in her hand. Should she or shouldn't she? She'd found it on the large ring with all the other keys in her Grandmother's desk, but it was the only one with a ragged piece of red yarn attached. It had to be special.

Memories lurk everywhere. So many special days, so many special hopes and dreams; Thanksgiving turkey with oyster stuffing, homemade cranberry sauce, pumpkin pie with chopped nuts on the bottom and whipped cream sliding off the top and best of all, dozens of sugar cookies with their names in chocolate across the top.

They'd arrive the day before Christmas, her father, mother, sisters and herself. The house came alive with their laughter as they set up the tree and helped prepare the holiday dinner. Katie saw herself, a child of six, sitting on the hearth cracking nuts; her tummy filling faster than the bowl. Katie was the only one her Grandma trusted with this delicate job. She hadn't realized then what a gift her grandmother had for filling her with pride and confidence.

The minute the metal clinked in the keyhole she knew it was the right key, but it wouldn't turn. Rocking it back and forth, like a dentist pulling a tooth, she felt it give. One determined twist to the right and she heard a click.

Grasping the brass tongue in her hand she pushed up. It was stuck. She needed something to pry it open; a screwdriver, a table knife, something thin that wouldn't snap and break.

She sat back on her haunches. Rivulets of sweat glued her thick blonde hair to her head. Katie reached in the rag pile behind her, grabbed a rag and dried her hands. It wasn't comfortable, her heels pressing into her buttocks, but now her eyes were level with the lock. She hesitated. She'd been warned never to open this trunk, and here she was, hands shaking, heart pounding, gulping like a fish out of water. Could it be Pandora's box all over again? She could always burn the letters in the back yard without reading them, but then how would she ever know?

She rummaged through the old lopsided basket at her feet and found an old kitchen knife which she slid under the tongue. It squeaked in protest but loosened it's hold. She pushed up on the lid. The musty smell of old paper filled her nostrils. Letters, bound in faded blue taffeta, lay atop a multicolored quilt. There was a loose piece of paper, like a page torn from a diary, covered with handwriting atop the letters. As Katie picked up one bundle of letters her fingers brushed the quilt. The strangest feeling shot through her, as if she'd touched something alive. She jumped, dropping the letters back in the trunk. Don't be silly, she told herself, there's nothing here but old letters, and an old quilt. Once again she reached down and grasped a pile of letters. This time she was careful not to touch the quilt. She held them in her hand as she gazed down at the quilt. The colored shapes were no longer vibrant but the quilt was beautiful, its pastel colors and fine needlework a pleasure to look at.

Sweat crept down her back like a woolly brown and black caterpillar. She'd come back later, when it was cooler, but she had to read one letter. She wanted to feel the closeness, touch the person who wrote it. The paper was as smooth and delicate as a butterfly wing, She cradled the envelope between her palms and held it, afraid it would turn to dust.

Katie picked up the loose page from the diary. The black ink had faded to light brown but was legible. There was no greeting, only the date, 1899 in the right hand corner. It began, "Rebecca was cruel to Emma." Whoever said that was a liar, and Kate knew it. She turned the page over, there was no signature.

Rebecca was Katie's Grandmother and Emma her mother's half-sister. Her mother always hedged any questions about her background, so there was no point in even asking.

Katie tried to remember what she knew about her mother's history: her mother, Roseanna, was born in Missouri and raised in Uxbridge, Massachusetts but why, Katie had no idea. The few family pictures she'd seen were of people she's never met or who had been dead for years.

Why had her Grandfather died at age forty-five? Her mother must have been five or six years old, but she couldn't be sure as her mother never would tell her age. Katie didn't remember taking flowers to a cemetery, so where was her grandfather buried? She wiped her face with the back of her dusty hand.

Over the years there had been so many stories. Could the answers be in the mystery trunk? Why would anyone go to so much trouble to lock up old letters? Why all the warnings? She straightened her spine and squared her shoulders. The decision was made, she would read the letters, but not until her sisters and mother were gone. Returning the delicate old letters to the trunk she closed the lid. Her hands were shaking.

After the usual farewells she stood on the porch, waving goodbye, then rushed into the house not giving the sun a chance to heat the attic. She picked up Cheese, a flashlight and a handful of paper bags . She hadn't told her sisters she'd found the key to the old trunk.

Squatting on her heels, Katie stared into the old chest. Somewhere behind her the cat knocked something to the floor. "Get over here, Cheese," Katie patted the rag pile next to her and waited for Cheese to jump down from the dresser. "Gram would kill me if something happened to you."

By nine o'clock the trunk was empty and the bags full. She made a second trip to bring the quilt downstairs and folded it over the back of the rocking chair next to her bed. She couldn't help but wonder who had done such beautiful work and where each swatch of material came from. The yellow gingham with tiny blue flowers, from a little girl's dress maybe. The light blue piece with the thin dark stripe, a man's shirt perhaps, and the two triangles of faded white satin. A wedding dress? Tomorrow she'd hang the quilt outside to air and get rid of the musty odor. The bedroom was beginning to smell like the inside of the trunk. She opened a window and let in the early summer smells.

Katie's head itched. It felt dry and dusty. She needed to clear the cobwebs from her brain. Her mind whirled with thoughts of the grandmother she knew and loved. What could possibly be in these letters that was so horrible?

Her shower over and the sun away for the night, Katie sat on the edge of the bed. A pile of envelopes sat next to her pillow, the rest leaned against the baseboard by the head of the bed. The cord on the window shade gently tapped against the screen. Cheese was asleep at the foot of the bed. Katie fluffed up her pillow and leaned back, her hand shaking as she opened the first letter.

Chapter Two

Rebecca swung her legs over the side of the bed, feet groping for slippers that seemed to have wandered away during the night. She got down on all fours and peered under the bed. Ah, there they are, on the far side, up against the wall. She looked more like a child than a woman of twenty-two years. She rubbed her green eyes, trying to rid them of sleep then pushed her auburn hair away from her face and yawned. It was time to get up.

Afraid of waking her two nieces, she didn't light the kerosene lamp so she couldn't see her breath in the chilly morning air. She shivered. Somewhere among the blankets at the end of the bed was her robe. Her fingers touched soft flannel. After tying the braided blue belt around her waist she sat for a moment, like a robin in a snow storm, shoulders hunched, knees held tight as she hugged herself, waiting for her body heat to find all the nooks and crannies inside her robe.

She tiptoed down the hall, avoiding the squeaky board in front of Robert and Anne's bedroom door.

She had the bathroom to herself. There was the faint odor of flowers; from the soap, probably. Clean, dry towels hung to the left of the water basin. She leaned against the old dresser, holding the basin and closed her eyes. Oh, the blessed quiet. No one wanting a hairbrush, no gooey soap melting in the bottom of the basin and no wet towels on the floor.

She looked at herself in the mirror and her mind began to

wander. She knew before she left Ireland that times were hard in New England. Politics were as confusing here as in Ireland with President Cleveland saying he'd have the country on its feet in no time and the Republicans saying it was impossible. Only time would tell. No matter, she felt safe and was fortunate enough to have found a job. Being here with her brother Robert and his family made up for any inconvenience, but she did miss her privacy and longed for a room of her own. With a new baby coming, Robert and Anne were hard pressed for space. She'd thought of moving to a rooming house but it would be an unkind thing; they'd think she was unhappy living with them, or worse, ungrateful. She was neither. Robert and Anne had done so much for her; without them she'd still be in Ireland.

She cleared her head of foolish thoughts. Grand ideas she had for somebody not an hour at a new job. Shame overcame her and she was unable to look at herself in the mirror.

Rebecca sat at the kitchen table reading as Anne took the last doughnut from the hot oil.

May 20, 1893

Dear Becky,

I was so glad to get your letter and know you arrived alright. I'm sorry you had such a bad trip, but the Atlantic is not known for calm seas, particularly in February. I'm surprised to hear there's so much snow on the ground. How far out of Boston are you? It sounds like I know where Boston is. I did find it on the map, but I can't find Uxbridge.

Your brother must have changed a lot, did you recognized him? I know I wouldn't, it's been so many years and I hardly remember his wife, Anne, and you met your nieces and nephew for the first time. How do you like them?

Have you gotten a job yet? There must be a family eager for someone as well trained as yourself even if times are hard over there.

Nothing new here. I saw your stepmother last week at the

general store. As usual, she ignored me. She was alone, but I have to admit she looked nice. Her dress must have cost a pretty penny, it had those new leg-of-mutton sleeves. All for grocery shopping mind you!

Write and let me know how you like it and what you are doing. Have you found a boyfriend yet?

Your friend, Mary Reagan

P.S. I forgot to ask if you've read the new book, *The Strange Case of Dr. Jekyll and Mr. Hyde?* It's scary, don't read it when you're alone.

Rebecca laid the letter on the table. The aroma of coffee, bread baking and hot doughnuts filled the room. She wrapped her fingers around the hot mug of tea, a habit carried over from Ireland when her hands were never warm. She watched as her sister-in-law' shook the last doughnut free of grease, letting the lard drip to the pan below. "Don't bite into it, Rebecca you'll scorch the inside of your mouth" she said as she rolled it in confectionery sugar.

The wonderful odors reminded Rebecca of home, before her mother died, and Robert and Anne hadn't left for America.

"Who's your letter from, Rebecca?" Anne wiped her hands on her spotless apron, her fair skin gleamed from the heat of the stove. Her black hair was parted in the middle, drawn back into a stern bun and held tight at the nape of her neck with hairpins. She wasn't expecting callers, not at seven in the morning, yet she was scrubbed and every strand of hair in place. Anne had recently replaced her apron with a clean one, but Rebecca did not know that.

Rebecca and her brother Robert had the same porcelain skin, but Robert's face was inclined to be ruddy from years of hunting and fishing. His curly red hair had allowed a patch of pink scalp to show, and peek at the blue sky above, as Anne affectionately reminded him. He cared nothing for clothes and despite hours of ironing and folding his trousers never had a crease and his shoes were scuffed.

"It's from Mary Reagan, back home." Rebecca shook herself free of her reverie and handed the letter to Anne. "We used to walk to school together every morning. You remember the Reagans. Her dad had a small farm on the far side of town, near Doyle's meadow, a nice little place it was."

Anne peered closely at Rebecca. "You aren't homesick are you, girl?"

This would have surprised Anne after Rebecca had waited so long to get to America; all of them working and saving to get her here.

"No, no. I'm eager to start work this morning, and more than happy to have the work to go to." Rebecca poured herself more tea and added a teaspoon of sugar. She looked at the doughnuts in the center of the table. "I've gained five pounds since I've arrived and it's not been more than six weeks. All this wonderful baking. What are you doing to me?" She sighed as she reached for a doughnut, licking the sugar from her fingers as she set it in her napkin,

"You'll be happy at the Tafts, Rebecca. I can't wait for you to tell me about it when you get home." Anne laid her doughnut on the table and blew on her fingers. "I never remember things being so bad here in Massachusetts, with the mills closing and all. Jobs are not that easy to come by. Mr. Blanchard told Robert the bookkeeper is the last to be laid off at the quarry, so Robert's job is safe for now." Anne reached across the table and patted Rebecca's hand, "The Tafts are a nice family, highly respected here in Uxbridge. You'll be happy there, I know."

On her way out the door, Rebecca stopped in front of the mirror, intending to make last minute adjustments. "No need for that, you're looking as slick as a race horse. That white blouse and brown skirt are a perfect pair, not too dressy and not too plain," Anne said as she started through the kitchen towards Rebecca.

"If you keep baking and I keep eating they'll not be fitting at all." Rebecca leaned over and gave her sister-in-law's shoulder a squeeze.

"It'll take a lot of filling to put a dent in that tiny waist." Anne's eyes glinted with mischief, "Come here, Carrot Top, let me help you with those wandering wisps of hair."

Rebecca's eyes flicked with anger, but only for a second before a broad smile touched her lips. "The last one to call me that has a chipped tooth to show for it, back in my younger days, of course, and I haven't been pining to hear it again, Annie Brown."

Anne brushed the hair from Rebecca's translucent check. As soon as Anne maneuvered the last hair in place Rebecca said, "It's time I was going." She pulled on her bolero jacket and fastened the two frogs holding it closed before tucking her new apron under her arm.

"Be careful not to drop your apron." Anne stood in the doorway. She would have had a waist if she hadn't been expecting her fourth child. She kissed Rebecca on the cheek. "I so enjoy having you here. I know the children upset you, but in time you won't even hear them."

"You'll be needing space with the new baby coming." Rebecca stood for a moment, a thoughtful frown on her face. "I'm so nervous. I know I'll do something wrong, and I don't want to disappoint you and Robert after all you've done for me." She laid her hand on top of Anne's. "Say a prayer to anyone you think can help," Rebecca's Northern Irish breeding came to the fore as she added, " even that pious gentleman in the Vatican. He must be good for something." It broke the tension and they both laughed.

"You'll do just fine, Becky. You'll find Bridie and Mavis good, helpful girls. They've worked for the Tafts for years." Anne paused, and smiled, a dimple showing in one cheek,. "You'll make friends, I know you will, and be sure and come straight home, I can't wait to hear what's happened."

Rebecca walked along the side of the dirt road, holding her skirt above the wet grass, her elbow tight to her side, hugging her new apron. It was a short walk, less than a mile but she didn't want the shine on her brown shoes to become scuffed or the hem of her skirt to have an edging of dirt. She stopped, closed her eyes, and took a deep breath. The world smelled green, of new furrowed earth, and fresh apples. Wildflowers peeked through the grass, a bit shy, as if afraid of a spring snow. The tiniest of dew diamonds sparkled among the bright purple, yellow and white blossoms. She stepped carefully, not wishing to disturb the colorful world at her feet.

Beyond the stonewall Rebecca could see the circular drive in front of the large, white pillared house. Wouldn't it be grand to go in the front way, she thought as she opened the door to the servants entrance and walked into the cozy kitchen, unaware her life was about to change forever.

Chapter Three

"Tell me all about it, Rebecca, I can't wait." Anne's best china sat on the shell pink tablecloth she used for company. She slid a warm slice of bread onto a plate and passed it to Rebecca. "Give it a chance to cool."

" I feel like company, drinking out of these cups and the tablecloth and all." Rebecca ran her finger around the rim of the bone china before taking a bite of the hot bread. "Oh my, but this is good, Anne, worth waiting the day for."

"Stop right now, I don't need you to tease me, haven't I Robert for that?"

Rebecca found it hard to sit still, she was as anxious to tell Anne about her day as Anne was eager to hear, but the urge to tease was irresistible. "Well, it took me longer to get to the Tafts' than I thought, due to the wet grass and all." She was unable to look her sister-in-law in the eye, afraid she'd laugh.

"Enough, Rebecca, tell me what I want to hear." Anne looked like a child at her first country fair.

Rebecca grinned. She hadn't the heart to continue. "Well, you were right, Bridie and Mavis were more than helpful. Mr. Rush, he's between a valet, butler and a handyman and his wife Kathryn, the cook, are both nice too. I was taken to see Mrs. Taft in what they call the sunroom." Rebecca set her cup in the gold rimmed saucer and looked at her sister-in-law. It was difficult not to smile. "Oh, and wouldn't it be grand to have a room just for the sun, one for the moon, another for the wind."

"Rebecca, get on with your story, Robert will be home soon and I'll not get the chance to hear it. What are your duties?" Anne sat forward, on the edge of her chair, waiting.

"Bridie, Mavis and I do everything but cook, but there will be times when we have to help Mrs. Rush in the kitchen." Rebecca giggled, "And can't you see me in the kitchen, I can't boil water without your help." She reached for her teacup and blew on the hot tea, careful not to spill any on the tablecloth. "The house is lovely, large rooms with wide board floors, windows you could walk through like a door they're so tall and low to the floor. There are fireplaces in most of the rooms and the dining room is elegant with a table that holds a dozen people or more, and all that silverware! Oh my, Anne I wish you could see it! It's almost more than a body can bear."

"I knew you'd like it. Not that I've been invited to tea, but I have been in to talk with Mrs. Rush. I've done baking when Kathryn had more than she could handle." Anne smoothed her spotless apron and looked up at Rebecca, a proud, shy smile on her lips.

Rebecca covered her eyes in mock horror. "And all this time I thought it was me they were wanting, and it's your baking they've been after." She opened her fingers a crack and peeked at Anne. The two women burst into laughter. "But I did meet someone interesting. A carpenter. His name is David Hawley." Rebecca let the sentence hang in the air, more a question than a statement.

"David's a handsome man. Been a widower longer then most, and him with all those children. I hadn't heard he was working at the Tafts."

"He's not; he does odd jobs around the house whenever they need him, things that need fixing. Mavis said she's made eyes at him, but all he's ever said is Good mornin' or good evenin' to her, that and no more. How many children does he have?"

"Would you like another slice of bread, maybe with that nice strawberry jam?" Anne leaned back in her chair and grinned as she checked the security of the bun at the back of her neck. "Two can play the teasing game, my beloved sister-in-law," she said with a broad smile.

"How can you do this to me? Tell me about him. I promise not to tease anymore, please." Rebecca stood looking down at Anne. She knew she deserved this teasing.

Anne smiled at her, a smile as sweet and innocent as a fifteen-year-old at her first school dance and said nothing.

"I'll get the strawberry jam," Rebecca replied, with a pretend pout.

"In the pantry, the shelf on your left."

Rebecca returned with the jar. "Last one." She set it on the table. "Tell me about him, where does he live, and how many children does he have?"

"I'm delighted you're interested, Rebecca." Anne waited for Rebecca to get comfortable before she continued. " Nice to know a good-looking man can catch your eye." She took a sip a tea, pleased to find it still warm. "Well, his wife Rachel and the baby died during delivery, so David was left with Jessie, Carrie, Sarah, Edward and Emma. Relatives are looking after them, all except for Emma. She's with David. Must be over six years now. He said it was hard enough giving up the other children but he couldn't give up his youngest, which I don't understand as they're the ones who take all your time, night and day. Such a blessing when they get old enough to help themselves. His sister Jenny helped him, they lived with her in the beginning. The other young ones are scattered about with aunts, uncles and cousins. He's a man who loves his children, so I'm surprised he hasn't remarried and gotten them back." She broke a piece of bread and covered it with jam. "Nice man, David Hawley."

"Did you know he's from Northern Ireland, too? Not far from Londonderry." Rebecca had listened in silence, not interrupting, waiting to hear all Anne had to say.

"His sister Jennie lives right up the street; Jenny Grafton, you met her." Anne began scraping crumbs from the table. "With a man like David, a skilled carpenter, a girl would have a nice home and

I'm sure he wouldn't want more children. A blessing in a way." She stopped and caught the crumbs in her apron. "You could do a lot worse than David Hawley."

"More of a blessing if he had no children and wanted none."

"You don't mean that," Anne laughed.

Chapter Four

December 8, 1894

Dear Becky,

I was glad to get your letter and hear you have a steady beau. Is he handsome? You didn't say anything about getting married but I want an invitation to the wedding. I won't be able to come but it would be nice to show everyone, your stepmother in particular. Remember how she always said you'd be a dried-up old maid? Bet you don't miss her, do you?

You sound happy living at the Tafts'. When you're married you only have to share a room with one person, until the babies come along. I doubt you will have a large family as you said he had children by his first wife. That should save you lots of trouble.

Aren't you glad I pushed you into starting a quilt? That will be the first thing in your hope chest.

James and I have finally set a date. We'll be having a church wedding in June. Wish you could be one of the bridesmaids. We have a little money set aside but will be living with his family until we get a place of our own. I'll be giving up my job at the Tierneys'. It'll be nice to clean my own house instead. James told me, 'No wife of mine is going out to do housework,' and like a good little wife-to-be I said, 'Yes, dear.'

We are busy getting ready for the holidays and I know you

are too. It must be fun with all of Robert and Anne's children. I'll be thinking of you. Write soon.

Love, Mary Reagen

"Merry Christmas, Rebecca and David." Anne held the door as she ushered them into the hallway. "Don't tarry, the wind will peel the skin right off your face." Anne stepped back and grabbed her long red skirt, holding it in place as a gust of icy wind billowed through the entry way. "Move yourself before I freeze. There's a lovely fire in the parlor." Still holding her skirt she gave Rebecca a hug.

"Merry Christmas to you." Rebecca returned Anne's hug. "I'd say from the noise, the children are enjoying it too!"

David reached down and helped Rebecca out of her heavy wool coat. "Wait till I put my mittens in the pocket, I doubt the walk home will be one bit warmer than the walk over here."

"Becky, you're a sight for sore eyes!" Robert picked her up as if she were still a child and gave her a hug to match his kiss. He extended his hand to David, "Happy holidays to you, David."

Kathleen and Ellen could be heard singing carols in the kitchen. The Brown sisters would never make a living singing, David decided, but they make up in enthusiasm what was lost in harmony.

David shook the snow from their coats into the kitchen sink. He was a tall man, over six feet. His muscular shoulders and chest were in a struggle trying to expand his jacket. His face was clean-shaven. He had a determined chin and surprisingly sweet mouth, high cheek bones emphasized eyes as clear blue as an October day in New England. His thick brown hair was parted to the left, curling over his ears and across the nape of his neck. He smiled easily and often, showing his overlapping front teeth.

Rebecca crossed the hall to the parlor and stopped, the room was a holiday kaleidoscope; silly, colorful, glittery, and childlike. The smell of pine eclipsed turkey odors drifting in from the kitchen. A loveseat, to the right of the door was a mountain of wrapping paper, satin bows and holiday ribbon.

In the front window, to the left of the fireplace, a plump red candle flickered from the depths of a magnificent cut glass bowl. Elegant green candles stood on either side of the bowl, their yellow flame reflecting in the polished cherry wood table.

Next to the fireplace, the Christmas tree sparkled and danced with light and color. Rebecca's eyes swam with tears as she recognized decorations not seen since her childhood. The boughs were laden with festive glitter and small candles.

"I've never seen a handsomer tree, have you?" Rebecca asked, unable to take her eyes away from the flicking lights.

"Never. It looks like it was born and raised in that corner," David replied.

Lillian, the blond, curly headed angel, smiled down from the top of the tree. Strings of popcorn and cranberry played peek-a-boo among the branches, and shimmering ornaments. Colored balls festooned with lace and glitter dangled from the limbs. The uppermost boughs had been hung with red and white candy canes. Candy canes that had hung on the lower limbs were gone, stripped clean by Captain, the dog, and Robert Jr..

Smoldering logs snapped, sending orange sparks against the fire screen and up the chimney. Three stockings remained of the six that had been hung from the mantle the night before. The children had eaten all their fruit and candy, leaving empty stockings wherever they happened to fall. It was Christmas and no one scolded them about making a mess.

Robert's stocking was filled with one large piece of coal. When they were all seated at the table before dinner he would pass it around for everyone to see while he told them how grateful Bob Cratchet would have been to have had it. Then he'd wait for the giggling to stop before a small voice would ask, "Who's Bob Cratchet?"

"Why he's the gentleman all bundled up at his desk in the corner of Ebenezer Scrooge's freezing office." And, of course, someone would say, "Who's Ebenezer Scrooge?" and so the story began.

"What a wonderful Christmas!" Rebecca held David's arm as they walked toward the Taft house, the tips of their noses kissed pink by winter wind—or was it the first blush of love?

Flakes swirled about their heads so thick and fast it seemed they could hear them. The new electric street lamps fluttered in the white misty snow. At the end of the street the spire atop the Congregational church was gone, swallowed up in the gauzy shower. "I hope they start leaving the lamps on every night, it's not easy to see when there's only the full moon, and it's scary with all the tramps about. There's so many of them, and they're so desperate looking." Rebecca slowed her step and looked up questioningly at David.

"They're hungry men, men with no work who have lost their families. I know how that feels." David looked down at Rebecca, a red and green knit cap on her head and her hands in green wool mittens. "They'll be getting a watchman for this part of town soon, although how much help one man will be if a couple of tramps attack, I don't know, but you're safe with me Becky, nobody's going to grab you — unless it's me." He put his arm around her waist and gave her an affectionate hug.

"My nose feels cold enough to fall off." Rebecca searched her coat pocket for a handkerchief. "I enjoyed the day at Robert and Anne's so much, even if the children were a bit rowdy."

"No more rowdy than others their age. You haven't been much around young people, Rebecca." David leaned down and smiled, "I'll be glad when my family is together again. I'm anxious for you to meet them all." David squeezed Rebecca's elbow, "Come, Becky, we're not that old, I'll race you to the corner."

"David, have you lost your mind?" But Rebecca had her coat and skirt in hand and was on her way before she'd finished the sentence.

"Watch for the patches of ice, I don't want you hurting yourself," he yelled after her. "Your brother will skin me alive."

Rebecca reached the corner before he caught her. "Now, Rebecca, what do you think the neighbors will say about that? You best start acting your age." His high spirits were infectious and

Rebecca laughed as he put his arm about her waist again.

"They'll have more to say about our hugging than our racing."
But David left his arm where it was as she leaned closer to him.

"Rebecca, do we have to go to the Tafts' for hot chocolate? I'd
like you to myself for a bit." David removed his arm from her waist,
and clapped his hands together. "The cold is trying to make a home
in my bones." The sharp snap of leather vibrated down the hushed
street like a bouncing marble in an empty tin can. A bony black-
and-white dog darted up the alley; head down, mangy tail between
its legs.

As they stepped off the curb, a sleigh filled with young people
glided silently across the snow packed street, the prancing horses,
leaving a wake of frozen steam hanging in the air. David hummed
along with the carolers.

"I don't feel a bit older than those young people, Becky. See what
you've done to me?" He smiled down at her. "They're on their way
to Ryan's Christmas party. They have the best party of the season;
the young people wait all year for their invitation." David held
Rebecca's elbow as they crossed the road slick with ice and snow.
"Last year they had hot doughnuts and cider, and we adults got to
taste that new concoction, hard cider. I'm not sure if I like it or not.
Afterward we sang and exchanged gifts. It was very pleasant. We
can go if you like, but we won't get a chance to talk together."
David didn't give her the option of answering before adding, "As
you know, my daughter Emma is with her aunt and sister in
Worchester so we'd be alone in the house, but there's no other
place, at least no place that's warm. Would you object to a cup of
hot tea at my house?"

"What are you suggesting, David?"

"I'm asking you to my house for hot chocolate, or tea, and
conversation. Nothing more." He looked down at her and smiled,
happy to see she hadn't been insulted by his suggestion.

"I have something for you, something I made that I didn't want
to give you at Robert's house, so it'll be fine as long as we don't stay
long."

Rebecca kept her hand in his, but had to jog in order to match his long stride. "Not so fast or I'll be needing my ice skates to keep up with you." They stood for a moment looking down the vacant street trying to see through the blinding snow. The soft glow of kerosene lamps blinked seductively from behind curtained windows and somewhere voices caroled "O Come All Ye Faithful."

"You'd think on Christmas day they'd be too busy to watch out their windows, but there's always somebody who'll be looking, so I can't stay long or they'll be thinking terrible things and saying them as well."

Chapter Five

David hadn't put up a tree. There was no smell of pine or baking, no candles, no decorations on the mantle; nothing to suggest a holiday. The house felt like a neglected child in need of a hug and a tickle. David shook the snow from their wraps before hanging them in the hall. He lighted a socket lamp and slid it into a holder on the kitchen wall before setting the kerosene lantern in the middle of the table. The flickering lamps sent golden globes of light dancing across the floor, walls and ceiling.

He filled the tea kettle with water and put it on to boil. Copper pots and pans hanging above the black iron stove twinkled in the mellow light.

A shawl of silence covered them, but they were unable to enjoy its comfort. David and Rebecca looked everywhere but at each other. They had never been alone before. A marathon of words spewed forth; a babble of nothing. Rebecca looked down at her lap surprised to see her fingers clenched into a tight fist. David laughed an embarrassed laugh. He reached across the table and patted her hand. "No need to be uncomfortable." He looked at Rebecca, a twinkle in his eye and grinned. "You make me feel like a young boy courting his first girl, not knowing what to do or say next."

Rebecca nodded in agreement but did not feel confident enough to answer. She walked to the counter, her back to him and measured tea leaves into the waiting pot. She cleared her throat. A nervous gesture, giving her time to think, maybe change the subject. "It would be a blessing to have the electric lights in the houses, no more dirty kerosene lamps to clean and fill every day. Do you think it will ever happen, David?"

"I'm sure one day it will." David took her by the hand, "Come, Rebecca, I'll start a fire in the parlor, we can sit there while we wait for the tea to steep." He stopped and picked up the tray with the cups and saucers. "Would you bring that little plate of cakes and cookies from the sideboard?"

"Did you bake them yourself, David?" Rebecca teased.

David grinned, "My sister Jenny thought Emma and I should have some kind of holiday together and put in some extra in case I had company. Maybe she thought you'd stop by, you and Anne and Robert." When they reached the front parlor he set the plate on the floor between the oversized cushions, indicating where they should sit. "It's not easy being a widower, Rebecca."

He lighted the kindling before sitting on the cushion next to hers. They stretched their feet toward the fire. Soon their laps looked like the ground beneath a bird feeder, crumbs everywhere. Their empty teacups sat on the floor out of their way. David turned Rebecca's face to him and kissed her on the mouth. She returned his kiss, not with passion but with a promise of more than friendship. They kissed again. This time he held her so close the raised pearl buttons down the front of her dress cut into his chest.

Rebecca put both hands up and gave his chest a gentle push. "David, I need more tea."

David leaned back and laughed. "We both do, Rebecca." He picked up the teapot and started for the kitchen.

"What is it you wish to talk to me about?" she asked as he started for the kitchen.

"I'll be back in a minute."

When he returned Rebecca was no longer on the floor but seated on the sofa, hands in her lap, ankles crossed. Her long, wool skirt swirled about her shiny, leather shoes, her feet not touching the floor, like a child. She gazed into the fire, hypnotized by the red and blue flames. Even the smallest of logs created a waterfall of sparks as it fell to the hearth. David handed her a cup of hot tea. He swallowed and his Adam's apple slid up and down in his throat as he stood, shifting from one foot to the other.

"Is something the matter, David?"

Rebecca thought he looked exactly like a school boy about to recite a poem he'd had to memorize, afraid he'd forget the words and be laughed at.

"Rebecca, as you know I have five children and I love them dearly. You've met Emma and you seem to like each other but I want you to meet the rest of my children. I hope you learn to love them, but I see no reason why you shouldn't, they're wonderful children." Abruptly he sat down next to her.

"I'm sure they are. Emma seems a nice child and at eight must be a help and of great solace to you."

David held Rebecca's hand in his as he moved closer to her, his other arm resting on the back of the loveseat. "Rebecca, have I told you how lovely you are? No, I haven't and I should have." This was followed by a kiss, not a friendly, harmless kiss, a forgotten-tomorrow kiss, this kiss held the passion and frustration of a man in love… yet unsure. He wanted this woman who made him feel like a teenager. He needed to hear her voice, to smell her perfume, to touch her skin and hair, to be wherever she was. And his children needed a mother, so why was he hesitating?"

Rebecca had never been in love, but knew she'd met the man she wanted to marry. She enjoyed his company, enjoyed his good looks, his laughter, his gentle teasing and his kisses. It was wonderful being in his arms. She liked the masculine smell of him, she liked the feel of his hands, the sound of his voice whispering in her ear and she returned his kisses with a passion that shocked and embarrassed her.

When he leaned over and kissed her again she put her arms around his neck, pulling him closer. She felt his hands unbuttoning the little round buttons down the front of her dress and she did nothing to stop him. It was wonderful to have him so close, to be alone with him, to be in his arms. She didn't want it to end.

His hand was inside her dress, caressing her breast. Her breasts weren't pendulous; they were the size of a small grapefruit. She hoped he wasn't disappointed. He continued to fondle her, pulling her closer, running his finger around the areola, as if it were the rim of a crystal glass. She felt the heat of his long body pushing against hers. When he turned toward her his aggressive hardness throbbed against her thigh.

He whispered, "Darling, we can stop now?" Not quite a question but not a final statement. He waited, but she said nothing. She felt him lift her skirt. Then his warm hand touched the soft skin of her inner thigh, and she sighed. She'd never felt like this, had never been this close to a man. What she wanted was to be touched all over; she wanted to be held. She made no effort to touch him, not sure what was expected of her. She kept her hands locked behind his head. She offered no resistance when he carried her to the bedroom and gently put her on the bed. She knew she shouldn't allow this to continue, knew it was wrong, and also knew the dangers.

But he had such gentle hands for a carpenter.

Chapter Six

As much as Rebecca enjoyed living at the Tafts', she'd return to her brother's house in a minute if there was room. She missed the laughter, the teasing and the unexpected hugs.

Rebecca walked, head bowed, unaware of the world around her. Dark circles ringed her eyes. Her skin was the color of putty. She had to talk to Anne. She had no one to turn to, certainly not her brother. Despair surrounded her like a cloak. She was drowning in shame and humiliation. For a woman as proud as Rebecca, a woman with a spotless reputation this could be the end. The end of everything.

She was at a loss where to begin, how to tell Anne. Her mind was a shoreline of words, churning like shells at high tide.

The wind had blown snow clear in spots, leaving hidden patches of ice. Snow scrambled up the sides of barns and clung to the thick bark of trees. Stonewalls hidden under a thick layer of snow, crisscrossed the countryside like fat, white dragons. Clouds whiffed across a pewter sky. Rebecca had never seen so much snow and hoped never to see it's like again.

Buttons of ice clung to the back steps of her brother's house. The long wooden handle of a shovel peeked from a snow drift to the right of the stairs. Rebecca didn't knock, knowing the door was unlocked, but stood a moment brushing her brown wool skirt as she stamped snow off her shoes. She removed her mittens, folded them in half and slipped them in her coat pocket. The brass doorknob was cold, but turned easily. The kitchen was empty, except for Captain, a half-breed German Shepherd, asleep under the kitchen table. He lifted his head when he heard her. Seeing it was Rebecca he curled back into a ball and resumed his nap. She removed her heavy coat, and breathed in the warmth of the kitchen. There wasn't a crumb on the scoured tabletop or counter. The room smelled of ham and potatoes roasting in the oven; it smelled of home long ago. Rebecca hung her coat on the peg by the back door and walked to the hall. She put her hand atop the newel post and in little over a whisper called up the stairs, "Anne, where are you?"

"Folding clothes in the bedroom. The baby's asleep, come on up," Anne whispered in return.

Rebecca tiptoed up the stairs. From the top step she saw her sister-in-law sitting on the double bed she shared with Robert, the bed lost beneath a pile of clean laundry. Rebecca leaned down and kissed her on the forehead. "Clean clothes smell so fresh, particularly in the winter when they smell like a cold, clear day."

"What a nice surprise, I'd enjoy a little conversation as I fold." Anne noticed the dark circles under Rebecca's eyes. "Rebecca, please sit. Are you well?"

Tears filled Rebecca's eyes. This wasn't what she'd planned; she didn't want to cry. She took a deep breath and waited for the pounding in her chest to stop. She pushed back from the edge of the bed and waited a moment longer before letting her shoulders drop. Her head felt as empty as a pauper's pocket. She looked at her sister in law but words failed to come. Anne took her hand and squeezed it. "Rebecca, whatever is the matter?"

Rebecca was unable to control the tears that ran down her checks.

"Oh my, Becky." Anne put both arms around her and began to rock and pat her as if she were a small child. "Oh dear, Becky, whatever has happened? Have you and David had a spat, are you ill, what's wrong?"

Rebecca dabbed her eyes. She leaned back and tried once again to say what she so desperately wanted to tell her sister-in-law.

"Anne, I don't know what to say, how to tell you, after all you and Robert have done for me. You'll wish me back in Ireland, I've brought such shame on you all." She paused staring down at the floor unable to say more. She looked at Anne. "I don't know what to do." Tears covered her face. Her small, hands twisted the sodden handkerchief, as if trying to wring it dry.

"Start at the beginning, the very beginning." Anne put her arm around Rebecca's shoulders, and Rebecca's head dropped until it was resting on Anne's ample bosom. Anne smelled of soap and lavender water. "It's alright, love. Once things get said aloud they don't seem so bad, saying them eases the burden." She massaged the back of Rebecca's neck. "There's no hurry to begin, and a good cry's been known to wash away many a problem." Anne reached across the bed and rummaged through the clean clothes searching for one of Robert's large handkerchiefs. "Use this, Becky, it looks as though you're trying to strangle the life out of the other." There was a strained smile on Rebecca's face as she took the dry handkerchief and blew her nose.

"I'll try." Rebecca relaxed and began again. " You remember when David and I were here on Christmas day?"

"Of course, the two of you looked so happy. How could I forget?"

"When we left it was snowing, it was such a beautiful night. There wasn't a soul on the streets, not one tramp, just a stray dog looking for a place to get warm. It was quiet and we'd come from having such a wonderful time and we were acting silly, like teenagers, and we raced to the corner. Then instead of going to the Tafts' for hot chocolate we went to David's house and had tea."

"What's so wrong in that? Emma was home by that time, wasn't she?"

"No."

"You were alone then." A looked of concern crossed Anne's face.

"David brewed tea and we sat in the parlor and ate Christmas cakes and he kissed me and I enjoyed it. I enjoyed it very much."

"Nothing wrong in that. I enjoy a good kiss myself," Anne gave a short laugh, "and I have four little ones to prove it."

"It didn't end with kissing, Anne." The handkerchief lay in her hand a wet ball, as tears continued to well up in her green eyes.

"Are you trying to tell me you're in the family way, Rebecca?" Anne stopped folding as she waited for an answer.

"I'm sure I am." Rebecca's one hand kneaded the soggy hanky as she wiped away tears with the other. "Oh, Anne, what have I done?"

"No more than half the town, I dare say, but that won't help now." Anne got up and shut the bedroom door. "The girls will be coming home from school and I don't want them hearing us." She returned to the bed and sat. "I'm going to have to say it and get it off my chest, 'twas a stupid thing you did, you knew the danger." Anne reached over and took Rebecca's hand. "Now, I've got that over with we'll work at solving the problem. Could it be you're late with your period? Many a time I lived in fear afraid I was pregnant again only to find my period was late." She patted Rebecca's hand. "How long is it since your last period?"

"Two months, and I'm always on time." Rebecca began to relax, the worst was over; she'd said what she'd come to say, she'd shared it with Anne.

"Did it happen just the one time?" Anne sorted through the pile of clothes until she found another of Robert's handkerchiefs and handed it to Rebecca.

"Just the once."

"Oh, dear God, why you?" Anne gave Rebecca a hug. "We've got to think." Placing her finger under Rebecca's chin she brought her face up so she was looking her in the eye. "And what has David said?"

"I haven't told him." Rebecca stared at the bedspread, unable to meet Anne's eyes.

"First things first, Rebecca, and the first thing is to tell David. He's an honorable man. I know he'll want to marry you. You have only to see the two of you together to know he's head over heels in love."

Rebecca got up from the bed and walked to the window standing with her back to Anne as she gazed into the backyard. Elongated lavender shadows rested softly in the virgin snow. "Anne, I don't want this baby. I'm not sure I want to get married. Everything is happening too fast." Rebecca turned and faced her sister-in-law, unsure if Anne understood how she felt.

"Rebecca, you'll love this baby. Listen to me, I know what I say. Do you think all our children were planned?" Anne folded a clean towel and added it to the pile at the end of the bed. "Would it be easier if I spoke with David?" Anne stared out the window, thinking. "We won't tell Robert yet, not till more's been settled. Men look at these things a little differently; it would be best to say nothing for now," she added.

"I don't know what I want, except I don't want six children. It would be bad enough if they were my own." Rebecca walked to the bed and picked up the clean pile of towels and set them on the bureau before sitting next to Anne, "I don't know anything about children except I don't want any, not even the one I'm carrying."

"You lost that choice, Rebecca." Anne stopped and looked at her sister-in-law's flushed face. She knew what Rebecca was thinking. "And don't think of getting rid of the child, abortion is dangerous, kills more girls than it helps. You're only twenty-three years, you've years ahead of you, don't be foolish and do something you'll regret or not live long enough to regret. I wasn't always happy with my pregnancies," Anne smiled at the memory, " but I could never rid myself of a child of Robert's, Robert loving children as he does. How could I leave him with a houseful of children?" Anne shook her head. "And the poor darlin' killing himself with work, to feed and clothe us all."

"I can't imagine you wanting an abortion, not the way you love children, and I thank you for offering to talk with David, but I can see now I must do that myself." She gave Anne a hug. "You've set my mind straight and helped more than you'll ever know and I thank you for that. This is the first peaceful moment I've known for over two months." The lines had softened between Rebecca's eyes, and her hands lay quiet in her lap. "The girls are home from school, I hear them downstairs."

They sat for a moment, listening to the girls talking and giggling downstairs before Rebecca whispered, "I'm not quite sure how I want to do it, but I know what must be done, you've straightened out the obvious. I should have seen it myself. Yes, I love David and that's what makes it's so hard. I don't want to complicate his life any more than it is, but I want a life too. I'm not sure a child is the answer for me, but I'm sure I don't want a houseful of children." She thought for a minute. "I couldn't contend with all five of his children. You grew into it one child at a time, with me it would be five children plus a new baby all at once, with no time to grow in between." Rebecca stopped for a moment. "And how can I be sure David wants to marry me? He might think the child is not his." She paused and sighed. "No, I doubt that; a woman can sense if a man will accept the truth." Rebecca sat on the bed and this time it was she who put her arm around her sister-in-law. "But one thing I do know—I'm fortunate having you for my friend, and I'll not forget it."

Anne returned Rebecca's hug. Trying to hide a grin, she replied, "And how can you be forgetting with me to remind you every day!"

Chapter Seven

Before Rebecca had a chance to ring the bell, the front door opened and David said, "Come in, Rebecca, how wonderful to see you." He stepped back leaving her room to enter the small foyer.

A woman's desk and an oak bench, the size of a loveseat, sat opposite each other on either of side of a braided rug. A mirror centered between four wooden pegs was attached to the oak bench. The upper right peg held a man's dark blue wool jacket, the bottom, a child's green sweater. A red rubber ball was caught between a pair of men's heavy winter boots under the bench.

"Good afternoon, David." Rebecca stood in the foyer unbuttoning her heavy wool coat. David held it for her as she pulled her arms free of the bulky sleeves.

"Anne said you'd be here at one and you're right on time." David filled in the awkward silence. He had no idea what was happening, what was so urgent. He didn't like having to guess and Anne had told him very little, only that Rebecca would like to speak with him. He could detect nothing unusual in their conversation. What was most puzzling was that he and Rebecca saw each other at the Taft house every day, and were together every Sunday afternoon, so what could Rebecca have to say that she couldn't have told him before? What could be so important?

He'd been especially careful that they were never alone again. He hadn't intended to have happen what did. If given the chance to repeat Christmas day they'd never have left the kitchen. He

FRAN SMITH

could think of little else after it happened, but as weeks passed it became a pleasant memory he hoped one day would happen again, but after marriage the next time, not before; but that was two months in the past. What could Rebecca want to talk to him about? It didn't make sense.

He hung her coat on one of the high pegs and took her hand in his. "Come, Rebecca, we'll have a cup of tea."

Rebecca pulled her hand away. "In the kitchen, David, not the parlor." She was unable to meet his eyes. She turned and started down the short hall to the kitchen.

"Of course, Becky, I've set the table," he replied, "and the water's on."

Mrs. Quinby, David's twice-a-week housekeeper, had left a meatloaf in the oven and a warm loaf of bread sat on the counter. The room was filled with wonderful smells.

Rebecca was silent as she waited for the tea to steep. Words did not come easy, but her stomach was no longer the swirling eddy of the past weeks. No balled fist stuck in the middle of her throat, and she was no longer fighting back tears.

She watched David pour the tea. His hands were not the large, coarse hands of a working man but were shapely with long, tapering fingers. His knuckles were free of hair yet there was nothing feminine about them. Rebecca held her cup as she put in a spoonful of brown sugar and stirred. David returned the kettle to the stove and sat across from her.

"Rebecca, please tell me what's wrong."

There were no signs of tears; they'd all been shed. "David, I'm expecting your child." She set the cup in the saucer. Then for the first time since she'd known him, his lips pursed with anger.

"Why did you wait so long to tell me, why didn't you tell me sooner!" David brought his hand down on the tabletop, spilling hot tea across the spotless cloth. If Rebecca hadn't been holding her cup, that would have spilled as well. "Did you have to go to your sister-in-law before telling me? Did you think I'd deny being the father? What the hell is wrong with you, Rebecca?"

"Don't you swear at me, David Hawley!" Rebecca stammered in a rage equal to his.

David got up from the table and walked to Rebecca's chair and laid his hand on her shoulder.

"I'm not angry with you, it's the surprise of it all, Rebecca. Why didn't you come to me first, not someone else... even your sister-in-law?" He ran his fingers down the side of her face in a soft caress before turning her face to his. "You've known for two months and never said a word, why?" His breathing softened.

"I couldn't believe it was true. I had never known a man before as I'm sure you could tell, then when I knew it was true I needed time to think, to decide what to do." Rebecca took his hands in both of hers. "I had no intention of keeping anything from you, David but I didn't know what to do." Rebecca smiled, as she squeezed his hand. "And I didn't know how you'd feel.' She released his hand and tears fill her eyes. "An awful feeling it is too."

"Of that I'm sure. I've been wanting to ask you to be my wife, but thought you'd refuse, we've known each other such a short time," he grinned, "but I can ask now, you'll not say no, will you?" He was down on one knee next to her chair, "I'm asking you, Rebecca Brown, will you be my wife?"

Rebecca couldn't help but laugh, or love him the more for it. "There are other ways, David, and I want you to think for a day or two, marriage is not something rushed into."

"It is, Rebecca, when a child's on the way." He stood, his hand resting on the back of the chair. "I've loved you from the day I first saw you." He reached down and pulled her to her feet and took her in his arms. "You aren't the first nor will you be the last to be starting a family before the ring is on your finger." He put his arm around her waist. "Rebecca, my darling, we don't have the luxury of squandering time, we have a baby who is mighty anxious to join us, so the sooner the better. Your being in a family way doesn't mean I love you the less." Putting his finger beneath her chin he raised her head and kissed her on the mouth. He studied her face, and noted the troubled look in her eyes, the furrows across her forehead.

"And I don't want you thinking of a way to rid yourself of the child."

He knew immediately he'd hit a raw nerve. "We have wedding plans to make. Where would you like to marry?" David held both her hands in his, his face a few inches from hers.

"David, I didn't say we'd marry."

"Of course we'll marry. Have you spoken to Anne about a wedding?" He didn't wait for an answer, "Nothing grand, a nice home wedding would be lovely, either here in my house, or with Robert and Anne in their home. Wherever you'd be the most comfortable, unless you'd rather something on a grander scale." David forged ahead with plans, not giving Rebecca time to disagree.

"I'll not talk with Anne until you've had a day or two to think. You've got to be sure, David. I don't want a husband who wishes he were married to someone else or worse yet, not married at all." If only we could go back to Christmas day and start over, Rebecca thought to herself, with us marrying and not having a child on the way.

"Time won't change how I feel; we'll marry as soon as possible— next week at the latest." He kissed her again.

"You have children to consider. I can't contend with a houseful of youngsters now. I'm throwing up all the time." Rebecca didn't give David a chance to interrupt her.

"I have a cousin in the west, in Ohio. I can have the baby there. No one need ever know." Her fingers fumbled with the sleeve of her dress until she found her handkerchief, tears had started down her cheeks.

"Rebecca, there are very few here who can't count to nine, so the sooner the vows are said, the better." He picked up her hand and rubbed her soft skin. "This is my child too, you know."

"David, think on it, make your decision tomorrow or the next day, however long it takes."

"I don't have to sleep on it, I'll feel the same tomorrow and the next day and the next." He looked at her, love and warmth filling his pale blue eyes. "I love you, Rebecca."

"We'll talk of your other children later." Rebecca reached up and kissed him on the cheek. "I'm not ready for this baby, much less a child for every day in the week."

"Rebecca, there are seven days in the week, not five."

"'Twould seem the same to me."

Chapter Eight

Rebecca couldn't find enough to do. The house was spotless, laundry hung drying on the clothesline, two pies sat on the counter and cookies baked in the oven. All the broken rubber bands and gnawed pencils had been cleaned out of the junk drawer and the kitchen smelled of soap and wax.

Black-capped chickadees tapped at sunflower seeds, making the bird feeder spin and tip at dangerous angles. Yellow goldfinch and scarlet cardinals danced in like flamenco dancers drawn by the castanet-like sounds of the chickadees, snatching a seed and leaving.

Rebecca was going to wash her hair. She had a bar of soap and a half a cup of vinegar waiting on the edge of the sink, but first the cookies had to come out of the oven. There was only one thing she loved more than cookies and that was gingerbread; not the taste as much as the memories—warm gingerbread with the lemon sauce her mother used to make.

She draped one towel across the back of the chair and the other across her shoulders after first tucking her collar inside her dress. She tried to bend over the sink. It wasn't easy, she was filled with baby. An elephant in a log rolling contest would have been more graceful.

Her arms and legs felt as if they had been stuffed with wet wool, they were that heavy. It was an effort to move. She pulled a chair away from the table and into the sun spot at the end of the counter and sat. The sun warmed her back as her hands rested in her lap. It was a fight to keep her eyes open, but she had to wash her hair. It was over a week since last she done it.

Seven months in Missouri and she was no happier today than the day she arrived. Not that there was anything wrong with Missouri, it was a pretty place with rolling green hills and rivers, there were many caves and friendly people, but it wasn't Uxbridge. Her heart ached for a cup of tea with Anne. Rebecca's gleaming kitchen spun before her like a colorful Ferris wheel as her eyes flood with tears.

Living with a man was unlike anything Rebecca could have imagined. She loved David but in many ways found this new world bewildering. She had learned to speak differently of her feelings to David than she did to Anne. It was like speaking a foreign language. Men were men and women were women, they just didn't think the same way. Sex had to be the deciding factor; males approached a problem from the left and females from the right. Rebecca grinned to herself; impossible to understand why a male couldn't seem to grasp the most logical things.

Rebecca towel dried her hair, dropping the wet towel on the counter. A clean scalp and hair made her feel clean, like she'd been soaking in a hot tub for an hour or two.

She closed her eyes and pictured Anne's kitchen. Ah, the smell of baking, the two of them at the kitchen table, a hot cup of tea in one hand and a piece of warm bread in the other. A longing engulfed her, so painful and acute she ached with it.

She placed a hand on her swollen belly. Why anyone would want to be pregnant she couldn't imagine, all that nausea, vomiting, swollen legs, and up half the night, emptying their bladder. Children were either noisy or hungry or had to go to the bathroom or were tired or needed a clean diaper or a bath or any of a dozen other things. It was hard to understand why parents became so attached to them.

Did loving a man always mean having a child? There had to be a way to stop it, but how when emotions swung so out of control? She and David had only to look at each other for desire to begin.

This child had yet to be born and how her life had changed. What else was in store for her? she wondered.

Rebecca removed a pen and writing paper from the stationary box on the counter. She hadn't written Mary in a long time, not since the wedding, and she had so much to say. She dipped her pen in the ink and began.

Sept 25, 1895
Dear Mary,

I have so much to tell you and with the baby due any day I thought I'd better write before you thought I'd fallen off the edge of the earth. I'm sure you're wondering why we aren't in Uxbridge. We left the day after the wedding and are now settled in a house in Bancroft, Missouri. It's not forever, I hope.

Our wedding was lovely. We were married at my brother Robert's house. He and Anne and the children, and David's daughter Emma, and his sister Jenny and her husband were there. Anne had the parlor decorated with ribbons, bows, pussy willows, all sorts of pretty things. It's hard to describe but it looked so pretty, and she'd baked and baked. You would have sworn the wedding cake came from a Boston bakery it was that lovely, and tasted even better. A few friends arrived after the ceremony to toast the bride and groom. (That's me, the bride!) The next day David, Emma and I left for Missouri. David's cousins had written saying there was need for carpenters here at the mill and we could stay with them until we got a place of our own, which is what we did. We were lucky to find an empty house in a matter of weeks. His cousins were kind and made our stay pleasant but I'm sure they were as glad to have their house back as we were to have a place to call home.

As you can see from the return address we live at the north end of main street. In the spring the dirt road that runs past the door is a lake of mud, in the summer a field of dust, in the fall a scrub board of deep ruts, but in the winter it's worst of all. Snow and ice, packed down by horses hoofs and sleigh runners make it worth your life to walk on . Oh, did I forget to tell you it slopes uphill toward our house, (downhill if you're going the other way, ha, ha). A great place for a sled if you're young. Children have a wonderful time sledding into town. Can't you see me starting at the front door and sliding into town belly first?

The trip to Missouri was not pleasant. Black ash and soot got into everything, even our luggage. The creases in our clothes were full of it, can you imagine! Our fingernails were outlined in black, and whenever I blew my nose, it was like my head was stuffed with charcoal (Remember how you used to tell me I had nothing in my head but air? well, you were wrong). Everything we ate or swallowed crunched, even the water.

The train was packed with families and the more exhausted the parents, the worse the children behaved, racing wild up and down the aisles. Of course, they had accidents, so they were either running and screaming or sitting and crying.

Anne had made us sandwiches which were soft and lovely the first day, but by the second day were as stiff as Paddy O'Brien on Saturday night, but without them we would have starved by the time we got to Bancroft.

And it was hot in the train. David had gotten two facing seats so I was able to put my feet up. Emma slept with her head in her father's lap. I was dying for a drink of cold water (we had brought water but after a few hours I could have boiled potatoes in it). There were no facilities on the train, only in the railroad stations, and I was afraid to get off in case the train left without me. I know how Jane Eyre felt when she finally found Mr. Rochester, I almost hugged the Bancroft railroad station.

David is working at a small mill. I'm happy to say he wants

to go back to Uxbridge too. There is a piece of property Robert is watching for him which they hope will be for sale in a few months. It's on the Mumford River. It's a lovely five-bedroom house with out-barns. It was a dairy farm, but the family recently died off . David loves horses (did you ever see an Irishman who didn't?) and wants a place where he can board and exercise them. He feels it will bring in enough to support us. It will be nice if it happens soon (today would be fine).

We are naming the baby Robert Charles after my brother and David's father. He better not be Roberta as I have my heart set on a boy.

Emma, David's daughter, and I grope our way around each other. She's a few months past eight years. Sometimes she's shy with me, and often sits in her father's lap. She sucks her thumb and sleeps with it in her mouth. I'd have thought she'd outgrown that long ago, but obviously not. She would rather I was not here and she had her father to herself, but I am here and I'm staying. Emma went into a tantrum last Friday evening when her father asked her to call me Momma (she calls me Rebecca). Her bony little fists smacked down on her hips so emphatically I could almost see the sparks. She stamped her feet and dust swirled across the floor. David told her to apologize, which she did, talking to her shoes the entire time. He told her to speak louder, and to look at me as she spoke. Again she apologized to her shoes, so he sent her upstairs to her bedroom. I'm sure this did nothing to endear me to her, but there seems no way to change that, and I do try, but I don't care much for the child. We are going to wait and see how I get along when the new baby comes before deciding what to do about the rest of his family. Honestly, Mary, I'm not up to all those children, they'd drive me crazy.

Robert and Anne are having an awful time with their eldest daughter, Kathleen. She's seventeen now, and obsessed with a young man they don't approve of. He comes from a good family, North of Ireland people, but since he's gotten out of school he's unable to hold a job, and even worse, seems to have no desire to work. He drinks too much and for some reason, Kathleen thinks he's wonderful. Of course, he's handsome so has no trouble attracting the ladies. It is hard to understand as Kathleen is the quiet one who got good marks in school, and has been such a help to Anne. I hope for Robert and Anne's sake, and certainly Kathleen's, this changes soon.

Please send pictures of your wedding, and let me know all that is happening to you. Have you thought how nice it would be here in America? Give my love to your husband Jim. You've got to meet David. He makes it all worthwhile.

Your friend

Rebecca Brown Hawley

P.S. Thank you for my material pieces, they arrived before the wedding. I've gotten some done on the quilt. I'm so big with this baby I can't get out of my own way and find it restful to sit and sew. So far I have a few north of Ireland and Uxbridge memories sewn together. Have you started your quilt yet?

Your friend, Rebecca (Brown) Hawley

Rebecca folded the letter and slid it into an envelope. She rubbed her outstretched legs, then massaged the small of her back. Sun and shadows skirted across the walls and floor in a game of hide and seek. There was a hint of fresh wax and soap. Nothing in any of the drawers or cupboards was unknown to her; it was her kitchen and yet, it wasn't home, she couldn't walk up the road to Robert and Anne's house.

A regular lady of leisure I'm turning into, she thought to herself. Whatever would Anne say if she could see me? She removed a bottle of milk from the icebox and poured some in a glass and set it on the table next to the gingerbread cookies. Emma would be home from school soon.

David and Rebecca's house sat on the corner of Charles and North Main, next to the Congregational church. It was a two story, white house trimmed in green, with a porch stretched across the front and the back. The porch ceilings were painted light blue. The twin maple trees guarding the front door were old and towered above the house. Leaves stroked the green shingled roof as lovingly as a mother tiger licking her kittens. The front porch was for socializing, the back for bird watching and day dreaming.

The park-like backyard had three flower beds, a quince and cherry tree, and a vegetable garden. One corner was shaded by an ancient apple tree. Two massive pine trees dominated one end of the yard which at this time of year was strewn with pine cones and squirrels. The water from the back door well was clear and cold, so crisp it was like biting into a fresh baby carrot Resting against the porch rail was a large, green bush. Rebecca was not sure what kind it was. A pair of white birch snuggled, like young lovers, in the far corner.

The past two weeks had been difficult. Rebecca struggled up the stairs to the bedroom. Her stomach had gotten so large she felt she was pushing a locomotive up the stairs. Now with the baby due so soon she limited her trips to once a day, no more than that. She'd be happy when it was over. How much longer could she put up with this unwieldy body of hers!

The first pain struck midway up the stairs.

She lunged for the banister. It was like reaching for a trout underwater, her hands slid off the polished wood. She dropped to her knees, held her breath and said a quick prayer, the smallest movement could send her backward, tumbling down the stairs. The step was too narrow to sit on. With a corner of her apron she wiped her forehead, then dried her wet palms on the sides of her skirt. The pain eased. Using the balusters for support she pulled herself to a standing position; legs shaking, feet unsteady. Ah, the pain was gone, but two steps from the top it struck again. Pink tinged water flooded the stairs, sopping her legs and clothes. The newel post was within reach, if only there was enough space between pains. It was getting harder to breathe.

The back door opened with a bang.

"Emma, is that you?" she screamed.

"Yes, Rebecca."

"Run, get your father, the baby's coming; bring Mrs. Harvey. Hurry."

Rebecca was on her hands and knees at the top of the stairs when she heard the door slam shut. The pain subsided as she crept toward the bedroom. Grabbing the bedpost with one hand, and the bedspread with the other she pulled herself up.

Her head had become a vacuum of silence. She sat on the edge of the bed, wet shoes staining the carpet, undergarments and skirt dripping onto the bedspread and the carpet below, and fumbled with the buttons down the front of her dress until they were all open. Rolling down her soggy stockings, she let them fall to the carpet, happy to be rid of the cloying wetness. While searching for the button at the back of her skirt the third pain struck. Rebecca fell on the bed, bringing her knees up as far as possible. The pains lasted longer now and had become more frequent. She was sopped, tired and frightened. With shaking hands she pushed her damp hair from her eyes.

Dear God, when will they get here? The pain was tearing her apart. She was having trouble catching her breath, she sounded like an asthmatic. Fingernails cut into her palms as she tried to keep from screaming.

Where was Emma, what was taking so long?

Having a child she didn't want, a child who'd filled her life with nothing but tears and here she was, once again alone.

Where was David?

Someone was humming one of her mother's songs. It was so long ago she couldn't remember the name of the tune. Her eyes wouldn't open, the lids were so heavy they refused to budge. The sheets and pillow case smelled clean and fresh, full of sun and autumn breezes. She lifted her hand trying to get it from under the covers but her hand refused to move. Was it caught in the sheets or had she lost all her strength? She wiggled the fingers on her other hand as she inched it toward her abdomen. Her stomach was flat. The baby was gone. A lump pushed against the small of her back. Her nightgown? She was too tired to look now, maybe later. The humming stopped.

"Becky, open your eyes." David's voice. Finally, freeing her hand of the bedding she reached for him, stopping when her fingers felt his denim pant leg. David held her hand, rubbing the back of it with his thumb. "Becky, you've a beautiful baby girl."

Rebecca opened her eyes. Everything was a blur, as if she were underwater. The blur dissolved and became David's face. He was in his work clothes, his hair curled tight against the collar of his shirt, like it did when it was wet, and he was smiling. "When did you get here? Did I have the baby all alone?"

"Emma ran to the shop." He chuckled and gave her hand a squeeze." We could hear her yelling long before she got there." He pushed a lock of hair from her forehead. "Do you remember my undressing you?"

"I don't remember a thing after the last terrible pain."

"You were screaming when I ran up the stairs, Mrs. Harvey right behind me, and in no time the baby was here." David leaned over and kissed her on the cheek, "Rebecca, you've done well, I couldn't be more proud of you."

"I want to see him."

"I'll get Mrs. Harvey to bring her in, but, Becky it's not a him, it's a her." David smiled but there was a note of apprehension in his voice.

"It can't be a girl, David." Rebecca held his hand so tight his wedding ring cut into his finger.

"Rebecca, the baby is a girl, not a boy."

Rebecca looked at him, stunned. "You must be mistaken."

David laughed a nervous laugh. "Rebecca, I know the difference between a boy and a girl, and, believe me, she's a girl, a lovely little girl."

"But he's got to be a boy." She waited, hoping he was teasing, that he'd laugh and tell her it was all a joke. Or maybe she wasn't awake and it was all a dream.

"I'll get Mrs. Harvey to bring her in. Once you hold her you won't be able to put her down." He looked at her, love and anxiety in his smile.

"Later, maybe, after I've slept." Rebecca closed her eyes. It couldn't be true. After all she'd been through, it couldn't be a girl. When she woke up she'd find this was all a dream, she thought.

"Rebecca, open your eyes. Now!" David gently slapped the back of her hand. "Hold this baby, look at her and touch her. Stop your foolishness. You've had a beautiful little daughter and you're going to love her the way I do. Sit up." David put his arm across her back lifting her to a sitting position.

"Not now, David, not now." Rebecca opened her eyes, surprised at the tone of David's voice and surprised to find herself in a sitting position.

"You can cry all you like, but you're not going to ignore your child." He set the baby in her arms. "Run your finger down her cheek. Lift her up and put her face next to yours." He reached down and raised the infant's face to Rebecca's. "Hold the back of her head, Rebecca, she hasn't the strength to do it herself. Smell how sweet she smells. Have you no maternal instincts, woman!"

Rebecca looked at David, a puzzled expression on her face. She's never thought of that.

The baby was warm and soft in her arms. David was right, she smelled sweet, like a bale of new cut hay in the warm autumn sun. A feeling passed through her, a feeling so new it had no name. She wanted to hold her baby, be alone with her, cuddle down in bed, her face close to her daughter's face, feel her warm presence. A new sensation flooded her, filling her with the satisfaction of a bowl of hot soup on a cold winter's day. It warmed her to the bone. She looked at her husband and smiled.

Chapter Nine

"It's a wonder my teeth haven't fallen out with all this bouncing." Rebecca sat on the edge of the buggy seat, Roseanna asleep in her lap. "Will we ever get there, it seems we've been bouncing down this road for a month!"

Robert Jr. stood braced between Anne's legs. The reins were looped about her hands, coiled carelessly in her lap. "And if your teeth fall out do you think we'd be blessed with silence?" Anne peeked at Rebecca from the corner of her eye, unable to suppress a grin.

"I know how disappointed you'd be if I ever stop talking, so don't you fret." Rebecca placed her daughter on her shoulder and very gently rubbed in a circular motion until the baby's eyes closed. "Can't you make this horse go any faster, flick the reins or snap the whip or cluck or — do something."

"One minute you want to go slower and the next you want to go faster." Anne gave the reins a quick snap but Beulah continued to trot at her usual speed. She reached over and touched Roseanna's little hand, "Roseanna looks so like David but there's some of you there, too. You're glad you have her. I can see it in your face."

"And I thank you for that." Rebecca laid the sleeping baby down in her lap. "It's hard to remember life before Roseanna, or David for that matter. I often think of the beginning, that first morning, my first day at the Tafts'."

Anne gave the reins another gentle flick. The only response she got from Beulah was a flick of her ears and tail, as if she were chasing a pesky fly. She didn't break into a trot. "This darn horse is like some people I know; no matter how hard you push they don't go a might faster."

"David has such plans for the farm and so much work to do. The barn needs cleaning and painting, and the pasture has to be cleared before he can board any horses. He's been like a crazy man these past few weeks wanting to get here."

Yellow shafts of grass peeked through the patches of snow bordering the road. Soon the snow would be replaced by Queen Anne's Lace and by summer time, blue corn flowers and daisies would join the Queen Anne's Lace until both sides of the road were a tapestry of color. Rebecca enjoyed the crisp air as she looked about her. White birch hunched together in adjacent snow fields, like frozen, half starved vagrants huddled over a fire. Since Rebecca's return three days ago, the sun has been a ghostly glob in a white sky, yet there was the smell of infant buds and new grass; the world washed, scoured and buffed into another spring.

Smoke-stained chimneys sat at opposite ends of the two story white house like a pair of generals astride their steeds, scanning the horizon.

The green shingled roof looked new, at least none of the shingles were missing. Shutters hung from the windows like drunks at a local saloon, each in a different direction. But it would take more than a few lopsided shutters to upset Rebecca. She was home, in Uxbridge, at the farm. Her new life was about to begin.

Surrounded by boxes and barrels they stood in the kitchen. Anne's eyes flooded with tears." I was so afraid you'd not come back, afraid Roseanna would be grown before we were together again."

Robert Jr. pushed a small wooden truck across the brown and white linoleum floor, zigzagging between cartons, doing the growl noise little boys do when they play with a truck. He was a sturdy two-year-old, with black hair and dove-shaped eyes like his mother. Anne held Steven, two months, his head resting on her shoulder.

"Roseanna puts me in mind of Kathleen when she was a wee one."

Rebecca looked down at the baby she was holding. "David is besotted with her. He looks for her the minute he comes in the door, and don't think she doesn't know her Dad when she sees him." Pride could be heard in every word. "She only wants me when I'm out of sight, and a good pair of lungs she has too." The smile left her face as she looked up at Anne, " Oh, and you wouldn't have believed it, David was such a sick man while we were in Missouri."

" You'd not know it today, he looks the picture of health." Anne set the baby on his tummy across her lap and rubbed his back in a slow, circular motion as he slipped a thumb in his mouth and closed his eyes. "Did you find out what it was, what caused it?"

"They gave it no name." Deep lines appeared in Rebecca's forehead. "He'd turn gray as ashes in the blink of an eye and be vomiting the next. Like an eruption it was and he'd go on retching, poor soul, even when there was nothing left to come up." Rebecca paused, remembering.

"What caused it, do you think?" Anne placed the baby's head on her shoulder and nuzzled him like a mother bear with her cub.

"The doctor had a lot to say, but who knows how much truth there was in it." Rebecca bristled remembering the conversation. "He told David he should be in hospital and David told him he wasn't about to hang up his fiddle, not in some God-forsaken place like Missouri, with none of his family about, and he had no plans for dying right then, thank you." Roseanne began to squirm and whimper. Rebecca kissed her on the cheek before setting her back in her lap again.

"The baby's rubbing her eyes. Let's put them down on the mattress in the other room. By the time they wake we'll have had a bite of lunch."

As Rebecca and Anne returned from the bedroom Rebecca continued, "David had two such attacks."

"Were they the same?" Anne asked.

"So they seemed. He ate the same as we did, so it couldn't have been the food." She leaned in close and whispered, "I'm that afraid he'll not be breathing when I wake in the morning, the attacks are so sudden."

"Are you sure it wasn't something he ate that didn't agree with him?"

Rebecca shook her head, " No, it was never the same. No matter if it was meat or a bowl of oatmeal, he'd have an attack." Rebecca reached for one of the smaller boxes by her feet and set it in a chair. "We were two weeks in the Missouri house when he had his first attack." Rebecca unwrapped newspaper from the package, "In bed over a week the first time he was." She removed a pair of nesting pans. "He couldn't keep anything down, not even a cup of tea."

"And the second attack? Do you think it could have been gall bladder? My mother suffered with her gall bladder and it sounds much the same; the sudden onset, the vomiting and all."

"No, they checked for that. His gall bladder was fine." Rebecca tipped a large china barrel on edge and rolled it nearer the table. "You'd never know to look at him he'd been sick a day in his life. When Robert wrote and told him the farm was for sale it was the best medicine he'd had, I've never seen him happier." She reached across the open barrel and put her hand atop Anne's.

"You've a good man, Rebecca, you don't want to lose him." She gave her sister in law an affectionate smile.

A pile of kindling rested next to the black metal stove at one end of the room. David's round oak table and six chairs had ample space in the center of the kitchen. Two sets of windows on either side of the backdoor looked into the back yard; the perfect place for a vegetable and flower garden. The ragged remains of a child's swing hung from the lower limb of a giant oak. Across the yard the Mumford river took a sudden turn, and swung toward the house before it gurgled it's way to the west pasture.

The women continued to talk as they piled empty cardboard boxes in the corner of the back porch. "Is Kathleen still seeing that young man, the one you're not too fond of?" Rebecca asked.

"She is and Robert is that upset, to think one of his daughters is involved with a no-account like him, but first tell me about

Emma. You've said so little about her and none of it good." Anne unwrapped a pan and set it in the sink.

"One day's good and the next not so good, but Emma seems happier now that we're home. I only hope it lasts." Rebecca tried to reach down to the bottom of the almost-empty barrel.

"Wait, Rebecca, you'll be falling in head first." Anne reached down and handed the newspaper wrapped package to her sister-in-law.

"My good sugar bowl." Rebecca carried it to a sink already bulging with china, pots, pans and cutlery.

"Does Emma call you Momma yet?"

"Oh my, no. That's a terrible sore spot with her." Rebecca rolled the empty barrel toward the back door. She stopped and turned to Anne. "She hates me as much as ever but she'd hate anyone who married her father. You wouldn't believe the stories she told the neighbors while we were in Missouri. David laughed and said we'd best start calling her Cinderella, she's that put upon. He says when she's older she'll understand and appreciate me. I don't have as much patience with her as I'd like but she'd try my patience if I was a saint, and I've no halo pinching my head as you well know." Rebecca left the barrel by the door and walked back to the table.

"She's an unhappy child," Anne answered. "Too many changes in her life and her no more than a baby. Having a new mother meant giving up her father. It's not been easy on the child."

"I have tried to like her, I'd be happy if it was so." Rebecca looked questioningly at Anne. "But how can I like someone when they hate me so much?"

"She'll feel differently when she's older; David's right." Anne gave Rebecca's shoulder an affectionate pat, "Will you be sending for David's other children now?"

"Not until David has horses in the stalls He doesn't want his children here and be unable to keep them. Once they are here, it's forever and I'm not looking forward to that." Rebecca walked toward the back porch, "The thought of four more Emmas is enough to make me think of running away from home."

Rebecca set the last empty box on top of the growing pile in the corner of the porch. She stood for a moment listening to the river and the churning life that surrounded it. Swallows swooped, filling their tiny beaks with sundown sips of water before the river turned black and forbidding. Cardinals jabbered to anyone in earshot, establishing their territory. The velvet purr of wings and the whispering of field creatures blanketed the backyard like a feather filled comforter.

"Tell me about Kathleen," Rebecca returned to the kitchen. Anne had lighted the kerosene lanterns. She was holding the two babies as Robert Jr. sat at the table munching a cookie. "All the boys must be after her, she grows lovelier every day." Rebecca's green flowered apron covered her from chin to ankle. The sleeves of her white blouse were rolled passed her elbows. "Sit for a minute while we talk of Kathleen."

Boxes had to be set on the floor before they could sit in the chairs. Rebecca leaned back, closed her eyes in contentment and waited for Anne to begin.

"Robert forbid her to see Ralph a few weeks back, so, of course she started seeing him on the sly. Ralph's barely able to get his lazy body out of bed except to spend the night carousing with friends. His father has threatened to throw him out of the house, but of course he won't." Anne worked some loose hair into the bun at her neck. "None of this makes any impression on Kathleen, poor child. Ralph has money for drinking, but none for Kathleen. He takes her walking around the town square if he's not busy. We've told her what life will be like with a man like that, but she's unable to see it, poor darling." In a voice more sad than angry she added, "How can she be such a foolish girl!"

Rebecca undid the strings on her apron and slipped the strap over her shoulders. She hung her apron over the back of the chair. "Oh, what a waste, a pretty girl like Kathleen, but she's just turned seventeen, a child she is yet. Give her a little time and she'll see for herself." Rebecca leaned forward. "I've been meaning to tell you, I heard from Mary Cronin," she paused, "that's Mary Reagen's new

name. They want to come to America, she and her husband Jim."
Anne rocked the babies as she waited for Rebecca to finish. "David
and I have asked them here, it would be a great help to us, and help
them get settled at the same time."

"You couldn't find more honest, hard working people. From
good stock they are." Anne picked up her apron and gave Rebecca
a kiss on the forehead. "Robert will think we've run off with the
circus if I don't get home, but I'll be back first thing in the morning."

Rebecca watched the small carriage out of sight, her back
aching, her feet hurting, and a contented smile on her face — if
only David stayed well.

Chapter Ten

"Robert, what are we to do?" Anne sat on the edge of a chair set back from the kitchen table, back ramrod straight, knuckles white as she clutched her cup. The hot tea was not calming her. "My poor Kathleen."

Robert stood, staring into the yard. "You'll not know how close I came to hitting that father of his, and it would've put a good ten years on my life let me tell you." Robert clicked the nail of his thumb and middle finger together making a snapping noise. He had been doing this since they found the note Kathleen left on the table.

"Dear Momma and Papa, please don't worry or be angry with me, I have gone away with Ralph. We are going to be married. I'll write soon. Be happy for me. Love, Kathleen"

"The nerve of the man, telling me my Kathleen egged on that no-account son of his." Sparks of anger shot from Robert's eyes. "The fruit didn't fall far from the tree there. Like father, like son." He pulled out a chair and sat but before the seat was warm he was back pacing. Robert was as jumpy as butter on a hot griddle.

"You know they won't blame their own son and who better than our little Kathleen? That lazy, no-good Ralph Eaton," Anne came as near a snort as was possible for her, "but he's their son and that he'll stay."

She was afraid to set her cup in the saucer, afraid her shaking hands would cause a chip "There's nothing that lazy, no-good, Ralph Eaton won't do, and what's Kathleen going to do when he's

61

gone off with someone else? Poor child. Much good it'll do us to cry over spilled milk." She sipped her tea. "What could we have done differently, could we have said anything to change her mind?" Anne fought back tears. "We could have banged our heads against a stone wall for all the good it would have done us." Anne looked at Robert, momentarily seated across from her. The tone of her voice was low and hesitant. "Is there no way to bring Kathleen home? Where do you think she is?"

"There's no way of knowing, my love, but we've got to try to get her back." Robert was pacing around the table again.

"Suppose she doesn't want to come home? She could be in the family way by now." Robert poured more water in the almost full teapot. "God alone knows where he's taken her."

"Well, he doesn't have money, so it can't be far. All Kathleen has is what she's saved from birthdays and Christmas gifts, no more than twenty five dollars, if that much." Tears rolled down her cheeks.

Robert patted her hand. "No more, Anne, I'll not stand for your crying." He took the chair next to her. "I'd like to drown him in the Mumford and be done with him once and for all, the no-good bastard ."

"Robert Brown! Stop your cursing, no matter how true it may be!" Anne's forehead ridged into a scowl. "Twenty five dollars will take them to Boston or New York. They've enough money to last a few weeks if they're careful and eat lightly. Then what'll they do?" She glanced at Robert. "Or what will Kathleen do? He'll not stay once he has to go to work and he's had his way with her."

Anger replaced the tears in her eyes. It wasn't often Anne lost her temper, for which Robert was grateful. Kathleen will not come home on her own, she's too much pride for that, they'll have to find her and bring her back, Robert thought.

Annie pictured the worst, Kathleen alone in a strange city with no money or way to contact them. A shiver crawled up her back and goose bumps covered her arms and legs.

Robert said little, but his mind was racing: Would Kathleen refuse to come back to Uxbridge? Would she be able to hold her head up, knowing the town was talking, and laughing behind her back? If she was in the family way, what about the baby? What would her husband Ralph have to say about the child? Robert couldn't help but smile, here he was making plans for a child that probably didn't exist and a daughter, who if they did find her, might not want to come home.

Anne got up from the table and returned with a pencil and paper. "We've got to do something. Here, you take this pencil and we'll write a list of people who can help. I'll wire the Warrens in Boston. Cousin Jane has always been fond of Kathleen. I know they'll want to help and the same to Aunt Lizzie Smith, her son-in-law's a cop in New York. He should be able to check things down there." Anne picked up the pen. "Don't just stand there, Robert, start writing!"

Chapter Eleven

David grabbed for the handle of the wheelbarrow. If it overturned, he'd land on the barn floor, but he was too sick to care. He dropped to his knees and crawled to the nearest empty stall where he collapsed in a bed of straw, booted feet splayed across the wooden floor. The barn spun causing him to feel nauseous. Cheese, the kitten, tiptoed up his chest. With ears up and head tilted she stared into his face, bright eyes filled with questions. His hand rested in the soft orange fur of her back. With her tiny sandpaper tongue, Cheese licked the back of his other hand. It was as soothing as a mother stroking the forehead of a feverish child.

David opened his eyes and stared at the window high above, in the rafters just below the peak. Spider webs sprayed golden in the summer light shimmered overhead. He was aware of muffled barn sounds; leaves whispering across the wooden floor as delicately as taffeta skirts at a fancy ball. Outside noises were distant, aloof as a dream. The sweet smell of hay filled his nostrils and he buried his nose in it like a pig routing for truffles. His mind raced like a bewildered rabbit in search of his warren.

He and Jim had accomplished much these last eight months, half the stalls held rental horses with three more horses arriving tomorrow. He hadn't mentioned it to Becky but he was going to build additional stalls in the spring. He'd talk with her later, when he was feeling better, but first and most important was the widening rift between Emma and Rebecca. Something had to be done.

Wedged between two females was worse than having no chair to sit upon or bed to sleep in when you're so tired you can't stand. Emma failed to understand he loved her. She was so busy hating Rebecca there wasn't room for anything else in her mind. Of course, she'd understand once she was older. At the moment, reassurance was a thin thumb in the dike of discontentment. He could have tiptoed through a spider web in hip boots easier than keep peace between those two.

In his mind's eye he saw Rebecca as he'd first seen her, walking in the backdoor of the Taft house, head held high, not looking down her nose exactly, but everyone knew she wouldn't be coming in the back door forever. A mite of a woman, small enough to take a bath in the barrel of a shotgun, his father would have said. The minute she entered a room, all eyes turned to her; she was that kind of person.

He loved her from the first and she must have loved him too. Why else would a woman marry a man with five children?

His mouth tasted as if it was full of rotten onions that have been soaked in vinegar. He jumped up and ran for the door, vomiting before he was out of the barn. He didn't want Rebecca to see him, or know he'd been sick, but that was where she found him, braced against the barn door, his face the color of the stone he was kneeling on.

He would never have believed he was going to spend the next two years in bed and or propped up in a chair staring out his bedroom window before death kindly came to claim him.

Chapter Twelve

Nothing but her pride would be bruised if Roseanna fell out of the apple tree, the limb was that near the ground. It was doubtful she'd fall, that tree was as familiar to her as the creaky boards she avoided when sneaking out the backdoor. Anyway, how could she fall, she wasn't a baby anymore, she was ten years old.

Homework was waiting but the smell of spring lured her outside like a bowl full of popcorn dripping with butter. The late afternoon sun had dappled a leaf pattern across her body. She had warm spots on her legs where the sun had been. Eyes closed, her mouth watered with the crisp smell of Macintosh apples surrounding her. Opening her eyes she looked up at a lazy white cloud almost within reach, then closed her eyes again.

There had been no time to change into play clothes before sneaking out the back door. With feet braced against the trunk of the tree, she was in no danger of falling. Her mother would scold if she slipped and tore her good school dress.

Roseanna had no one to play with, Emma was too busy giggling with her girl friends to pay much attention to her anymore. Whenever George McDuff's name was mentioned Emma would hide her blushing face behind her nail-bitten hands. Next year Emma will be out of school and probably marry him, Roseanna thought in disgust.

Roseanna always knew Emma and her mother didn't like each other. She could hear it in their voices, in the way her mother cleared her throat, the way Emma turned on her heel and switched out of the room, but Roseanna was glad Emma lived with them, she'd always loved her.

She was able to see anyone coming or going on the road to her house but no one thought to look up at the orchard, so she was seldom seen dreaming in the apple tree. It was a prefect hiding place, a perfect dreaming place. She spent hours in those old gnarled trees, watching the clouds, the birds or sometimes a little ant scurrying up the trunk.

Roseanna could be a statue carved into the wood of the tree. Even the birds were so used to her they treated her like a branch, landing near her braced feet or outstretched arms. She must have dozed because the shadows had become longer and the cicadas were quiet. The distant cawing of a crow sent shivers down her back, it sounded like the wail of a train in the middle of the night. The voices of the squirrels no longer squealed, they, too were preparing for bed.

From the tree Roseanna could see dust rising like a ghost in flight, racing behind her Aunt's carriage. Aunt Anne was alone in the buggy. That was odd. The buggy careened to a sudden stop in front of her house. That was odd too, Aunt Anne always parked the buggy at the side of the house and went in through the back door. Roseanna held her breath as her Aunt leaped from the buggy. It wasn't easy for a woman in her seventh month of pregnancy.

Roseanna dropped down through the branches, good dress forgotten and ran through the orchard to her house. When she rounded the back of the house and was almost to the kitchen door she heard her aunt crying. More like sobbing. Her mother was murmuring words so low she couldn't make them out.

Stepping inside was cooler but it felt different, the warm feeling of home had disappeared. It felt like the day Papa died.

Roseanna remembered her Papa well. She remembered him propped up in bed or sitting in a chair, wrapped in a blanket looking out the window. He never tended the farm or the horses with Uncle Jim anymore. She remembered sitting in his lap and he'd blow warm smoke in her ear when she had an earache; that was long before he became so weak he couldn't even hold his pipe. He'd tell her stories of kings and princess, magic carpets, giants and tiny people and animals that talked, and he could whistle. He tried to teach her but she always sounded more like a leaky balloon than a melodic flute.

Roseanna, was six years old when her papa died. For months after she'd expected to find him in his room, or sitting up in the chair but he was never there and she was afraid to ask anyone if he'd come back. She couldn't ask her mother; she cried whenever his name was mentioned.

She stood for a moment on the back porch wondering and listening. Maybe something had happened to one of her cousins or Kathleen's baby. The only time Aunt Anne cried was when somebody'd died, but nobody'd been sick. It was probably Ian, Kathleen's baby; he was almost three now, he could have fallen or gotten hurt. Uncle Robert was never sick, so it couldn't be him.

Roseanna pulled the door open and stepped into the room. Aunt Anne was standing in front of the kitchen table crying. Her mother was holding her, and talking to her but Roseanna could only hear the crooning of her mother's voice, not the words. The women did not hear her enter. "What's the matter, Momma?"

"Go up stairs and change your clothes." Rebecca lowered Anne into a chair. She gave Roseanna a weak smile. "Your Uncle Robert's had an accident."

"Is he okay?" Roseanna shifted from one foot to another, hands clasped behind her back.

"Just do as you're told." Rebecca spoke in a low voice, all the while rubbing Anne's back and shoulders. She looked down at her sister-in-law. "Is Kathleen with the children, Anne?"

Roseanna dashed upstairs, pulling her dress and slip over her head in one motion. She dropped them on the floor behind the bedroom door. Her school shoes were shoved to the back of the closet after slipping into her scuffed play shoes . She didn't bother to tie the laces. Pulling her play dress over her head she raced down the stairs to the kitchen. Her mother and Aunt were still sitting at the kitchen table but someone had put water in the teapot and it was beginning to whistle.

Her mother's hand was atop Aunt Anne's. Two teacups sat on the table next to the milk and sugar bowl. Both women were silent.

Roseanna could feel the heavy, suffocating grief and her own breathing became shallow. A screaming silence replaced her thoughts. She was afraid she was going to be sick to her stomach.

Neither woman looked up as Roseanna pulled a chair closer to the table.

"Roseanna, go in the other room and do your homework."

"I'd rather stay here and have a cup of tea." Roseanna's clasped hands rested in her lap. "Can I have a cup of tea, I'll be real quiet. I won't say anything."

"May I, not 'can I.'" Rebecca said, unaware of doing something as mundane as correcting her daughter's English while Robert, her only sibling, lay dead in the funeral parlor.

Aunt Anne reached across for Roseanna's hand. "Let her stay, Rebecca. Don't push the child away, she's old enough."

Rebecca got up and poured tea in their cups. She stared at Roseanna for a moment, a questioning expression on her face. "Your Uncle Robert was killed in an accident today. He's dead, like your Papa, poor soul."

"Will I see him again?" Roseanna asked, looking at Anne.

Tears streamed down Anne's red blotched face. "No, my darling, you won't see him again, only the good Lord will be able to do that," She turned to her sister-in-law.

"Rebecca, whatever will I do without Robert, the best man who ever lived?"

Rebecca reached for Anne's cup. "Drink your tea and get yourself a cup, Roseanna. As soon as you've finished you're to go outside and play or up to your bedroom to do your homework."

Roseanna held her cup as her mother poured. It was like after Papa died. It was terrible, nobody was able to look her in the eye, not even her teacher. The kids picked their fingers, chewed on a pigtail, stared at their shoes, shuffled their feet, mumbled something and got away as soon as they could, like she had some horrible disease. They felt sorry for her, she knew that, but Roseanna didn't want anyone feeling sorry for her.

Over four years ago it was, and no matter how hard she tried she couldn't see her father's face anymore. There were pictures of him on the fireplace and in her mother's bedroom so she wasn't likely to forget him. She wondered if her mother could see his face when she thought about him.

Between shaky breaths, Anne sipped her tea. "I don't know what we're going to do. Me with a baby due in two months. Kathleen home again with little Ian, which I'm glad of, but how will we manage?" Anne buried her head in her hands and sobbed. "Poor, dear Robert."

Rebecca patted her hand, "We'll find a way…later." Rebecca turned to Roseanna, "Out the door with you. Your aunt and I have to talk."

Roseanna picked up her cup and set it in the sink. She stopped and turned to her aunt and mother. "I'll be right outside, in case you need me."

Chapter Thirteen

The eternal cup of tea was close at hand as Rebecca and Anne sat at Anne's kitchen table. No one had smiled since Robert's death. For a family that enjoyed a good laugh that was difficult and added to the stress. Anne's sallow skin was the same shade gray as the slate that had caused her husband to fall to his death a month ago.

Robert never saw the carelessly dropped piece of slate that caused his fall. Anne shook her head in wonder, "So simple a thing, and look what it's done to our lives."

"Upstairs with you. You'll be needing all your strength." Rebecca collected the dirty dishes as hot water filled the sink. "The baby's due in a few weeks." Rebecca turned and looked at Anne. "There's nothing more wonderful than a baby in your arms, so soft and sweet to smell and cuddle."

Anne responded with a weak smile. "I keep remembering the funeral. Reverend Chamberlain spoke so nicely, don't you think?"

"He did that," Rebecca agreed.

"Robert would be that ashamed of me. " Anne sighed. "Just think, this poor babe will never know its dad, not one memory of him." Anne leaned against the table.

Her enlarged stomach made it impossible to get too close. "I know I mustn't dwell on it, but something's got be done if we want a roof over our heads." Anne paused. "I've been thinking and have an idea. No matter how crazy it sounds I don't want you laughing or saying no. Think on it before you say anything, don't cast it aside without a little thought."

Rebecca set the dirty dishes in the hot soapy water and returned to the table. Anne had a need to talk and it would do no harm to listen. "I'll try not to but I'd welcome a good laugh. It will be nice to get back to normal. For the children if nothing else."

"You know how I love to bake and I've taught you what I know and you know I help when the Tafts have company and they'd not ask if it wasn't tasty." Anne lowered her eyes, embarrassed and proud. She wet her forefinger and began picking at the crumbs on the tablecloth.

Rebecca nodded in agreement.

"Why can't we open a bakery right here in this house? There's not a one in Uxbridge or Worchester for that matter. We could have the store here, in the house, right on Main street. I'll bake here and you and Mary bake at the farm. Of course, you'd have to want to do it. Kathleen can drive the buggy to the farm and pick up your baked goods. It would only take a half an hour or so. Add your baked goods to mine and we should make a fair living." She sipped her tea and waited. "Well, what do you think?"

"I'll have to sleep on it, Anne." Rebecca's mind was churning. It was exciting, this idea of Anne's. With her two older girls to help, and she and Mary baking on the farm, it could work. She couldn't help but wonder what the town folks would have to say, two women opening a business!

But where was the money to come from? She couldn't mortgage the farm; it was the only thing she had and where would we go if she lost it? Jim had room to board more horses if they could find a hired hand. I could let out that unused pasture on the south side, away from the house, it wouldn't bring in much but every little bit counts. "It'll take money to start. Staples and sugar aren't free, nor is fuel for the ovens, or a carpenter to make the front room into a shop, We'll be needing shelving and cases for the bread and rolls. So many things."

"Robert and I have a little put aside. I'll mortgage the house, but

I can't do all the baking and selling alone." Anne couldn't stop talking. "Think about it, Becky, it can work, it really can. The worst that can happen is we're a little poorer and have to live together at the farm or the poor house. If we don't take the chance we'll lose everything." Anne leaned back in the chair, shoulders drooping, back bent, hands resting in her lap. She'd finally said it, what she'd been thinking this past week. Now it was up to Rebecca. "Rebecca, don't discard it out of hand. I see it in my dreams every night, it can be done." Anne's look was one of desperation. "As long as we work together, and you and I have always been good at that. The children are old enough to help, even Roseanna can help in the store and run errands."

"I'll talk to Mary and be back in the morning. I'd not have been able to keep the farm if it wasn't for Jim and Mary." She took Anne's hand. "Now upstairs to rest, you look dog tired. And, Anne, I'm excited about your idea. We'll talk more tomorrow."

Chapter Fourteen

"Telephones, telephones, how could we get along without them?" Anne pushed her chair away from the desk. "Telephones, phonographs, motor cars, Kodak cameras, radios, what else do you suppose is in store for us! How far we've come these last few years."

Rebecca set her pencil on the desk. They were in the converted office she and Anne shared at the farmhouse. It had been the sewing room. It now held two desks, two chairs, an overstuffed filing cabinet and one small wastepaper basket.

"I'm going to buy a radio," Rebecca announced

Anne looked at her, amusement on her face. "Whatever for?"

"I'm thinking of putting an ad on the local station. You've heard the one Grey's Grocery has: potatoes on sale, fresh tomatoes, things like that. We'll still use the flyers and ads in the newspaper but this could stir up a little more business, particularly once we open the restaurant."

"Sounds like a good idea." Anne looked at Rebecca in amazement. "When do you get time to think of these things? My mind's so full of recipes and accounting there's not room for much else."

"Don't try and fool me, I know what your mind is capable of." Rebecca's eyes gleamed as she made plans. "I'll make up some new flyers and a new ad for the Uxbridge Times and we'll need another ad when the restaurant opens." Rebecca tilted her head to one side, indicating with a nod of her head, she said, "Bring your chair over and we'll start a list of things we've got to do. Once Gert gets here there'll be no time."

"What time is she's coming?"

"About ten thirty, any minute now."

Gert Snyder was Uxbridge's real estate-insurance agent, piano teacher and only divorcée. A desk and piano in one corner of her living room served as both office and music studio. She'd lived alone in the bungalow since her divorce from Stanley.

"How're things going for you two, bakeries not keeping you busy enough?" Gert asked as she breezed into their office.

Gert's hair shone like a new copper penny. If left alone it would shine like a pewter plate. Her hips were as wide as her shoulders. From knee to toe she was solid, no ankle could be seen. Her ankles and knee joints had exactly the same measurements. She never strolled or walked, she marched.

"We're on our way to the Bannister place. You remember Jane, was in the class ahead of us, lives in Boston now? Married some professor. Anyway, she wants to rent out the house. It should make a good restaurant, two large rooms downstairs, each with a fireplace, a big kitchen, and it's not far off the main road with plenty of room to park. Even has a few nice Macintosh trees in the back yard."

Anne whispered to Rebecca, "Talk, talk, talk. Poor Stanley probably said more the first week he left than the ten years they were married."

"How long has it been empty, Gert?"

"Not long, you're the first to look. Jane will sell if you offer enough. Come to think of it, she'd probably sell if you didn't. Be foolish of you though, wait till you find out how you like it, but it's up to you." Gert turned her attention to Anne. "How's that grandson of yours, Ian? Saw Kathleen in the bakery the other day, just as pretty as ever. Don't worry, she'll marry again, who could resist a face like that?" Gert laughed. "Even if she does have a child."

"Shall I push her down the stairs or do you want to?" Rebecca whispered.

Anne glared at her as she struggled not to grin. "Will you please shut up, we've got a lot to do."

"Home again," Rebecca reached down and untied her shoes. "Well, what do you think, did you like the house?" She leaned back in her chair and looked across the desk.

"Almost perfect. Lots of parking, pretty porch and the stained glass in the front door is lovely." Anne slipped her feet out of her shoes. "The bathroom downstairs is small, about right for a restaurant, and the kitchen's a good size, even room to expand if we need more space. We could put a few tables out on the porch in the summer."

"What do you think of a cozy bar in one corner of the large dining room? Good money as long as you're not addicted to the merchandise and the bartender doesn't have sticky fingers." Rebecca stopped, a puzzled looked on her face. "It's got a lot against it too; let's think about it some more."

Anne sat listening to Rebecca, a look of amusement on her face.

"The kitchen needs a bit of doing, a larger refrigerator and a few more preparation tables. The pantry has plenty of room but do we need storage more than cooking space?" Rebecca changed subjects faster than a rabbit zigzagged trying to escape a fox. " We shouldn't have any trouble borrowing money, the bank knows we're good for it." She wiggled her toes and massaged the back of her heel. "Wonder why it feels so good to take your shoes off?"

"It's that wild Irish blood trying to go back to the barefoot days when we ran wild on the moors." Anne became serious. "Are you sure you're satisfied with the house? We don't want to jump into something and be sorry later."

"Twenty dollars a month is a dear price but Gert says she'll take a bit less. We'll need a lease, we don't want her selling it out from under us. I'll talk to Richard about it and also ask if he knows any good chefs." Rebecca stretched her legs and relaxed in the chair, "I'll be talking to him later today. He just might know of a chef, he's pretty observant when it comes to things like that." Rebecca's feet groped under the desk searching for her shoes.

"A wonder he didn't remarry, having a son to raise, must have been too busy with his law practice."

"His wife died about the same time as David so it's been fifteen years or more."

Anne wasn't interested in Richard. Her mind wandered back to the start of their businesses and continued back to the birth of Roseanna. "Remember how disappointed you were when you had Roseanna instead of a boy?"

"For heavens' sakes, what's that got to do with anything?"

Anne knew how dear Roseanna was to her mother. "What would we have done without our daughters? None of this would have been possible without the girls."

"You should have had a dozen daughters, no doubt about that." Rebecca looked at her through lowered lashes but Anne refused to acknowledge Rebecca's gibe as she continued to reminisce.

"I wish you could have seen Kathleen load the buggy every morning, filled with children for the drive to the farm," she giggled, "what a sight, her two younger brothers holding on for dear life as they bumped down the road. Then back she'd come, wagon filled with baked goods and more children than when she'd left, the farm kids wedged in among the boys. It's a wonder they're not still pulling out splinters." She dropped her hand in her lap. "I miss those trips; it was fun just watching them pull up in front of the house." Her voice trailed off. "Becky there's something I've been meaning to ask. You haven't mentioned Emma in some time; how are things between you two? "

Rebecca thought for a moment, not saying anything. "She's no different now that she's married. I don't know if she's happy or not; she doesn't say and she'd as soon tell me it's none of my business if I asked."

"Does Roseanna visit her often?"

"Often enough; there's a bond there." Rebecca pondered for a moment. "It's not easy my feeling the way I do about her." She looked up at Anne. "You've heard what she's been saying lately, haven't you?"

"Not that I recall." Anne had heard but thought it better to say nothing, it would only add more fuel to the fire.

"She's still telling people her father was well until he married me. Hinting I had something to do with his death. Why she persists after all these years I don't know." Rebecca's throat tightened, "Of course she laughs when she says it, but she means every word." Rebecca shook her head. "One day she'll go too far and when she does it'll be the last time she sets foot in my house or Roseanna in hers."

"She wouldn't say anything to Roseanna, she has more sense than that."

"I've done more for that girl than her blood relatives and gotten a swift kick for my efforts."

"Maybe you should try talking to her again."

"Talk to her? I'd get more response from the ironing board than I'd get from her." Rebecca pulled at a hangnail.

Anne looked closely at Rebecca. Her red hair had lost none of its shine. She had skin as smooth as vanilla ice cream and eyes as clear as Crystal Lake on a July day. Men stared when she passed by, so it wasn't lack of attention that kept her single.

"You've never been overly fond of children, Rebecca, and I'm sure Emma felt that. You tried hard, I give you that, and she was a difficult child. When next I see her I'll speak with her again and see if I can't make it a bit easier for the two of you."

"Say nothing to her, Anne. She should have married a man from Ireland; at least she'd be a good distance away." Rebecca continued playing with the offending hangnail. "The two babies don't leave her much time for mischief, at least for now. Speaking of daughters, is Kathleen thinking of remarrying? She's been seeing a lot of Josh Reynolds these past few months." Rebecca drew circles on a piece of scrap paper. "He's a bit old for her, don't you think?"

"Eighteen years older, a widower over three years now, poor soul, married less than a year and his young wife dead of appendicitis."

Anne hunched her shoulders as she shook her head. "It's hard to tell how serious Kathleen is. A good husband he'd make and a fine father for Ian. He has no children from his first marriage and he's ambitious." Anne ran her tongue over her lips. "It would be a blessing if Kathleen marries. That no-account first husband has never so much as sent Ian a birthday card. Going on four years since she came home, poor child." She paused for a moment, "She needs a man who'll take care of her and Ian. She's too young to spend the rest of her life alone. If she marries Josh they'll stay here, all his business interests are in Uxbridge." She gave Rebecca a moment to digest this information. "This last summer Josh rented boats on the river. Half a dozen or more. He's doing well, so he says, hopes to have five more in the water before the church picnic in June. He's clearing land on the far side of the common for a picnic area. Swings and seesaws for the children, and a booth to sell lemonade and ice cream. I've never had any, have you?" Not giving Rebecca a chance to answer, she continued, "He's setting in horseshoe pins and has plans for a baseball diamond. His property sits right on the water's edge." Anne leaned back in the chair. "Of course, it's only open on Saturdays now but he'll be open all week once the weather gets warmer. Beside all that he's busy with his lumberyard north of town... ambitious man, Josh."

"Now that I know Kathleen's taken care of, what about you? You're a young, handsome woman." Not realizing she was foretelling the future, Rebecca asked, "Have you any thoughts of marrying again?"

"Between my children and you where would I get the time to think?" Anne laughed.

"One day the children will be gone and there'll be just you and me," Rebecca teased, "Isn't that enough to scare you into marriage?"

Anne thought before answering. "I promise to think on it, if I get a chance," and added, "there's a good man out there waiting if you sit long enough for him to grab you."

"So I can have more children, and someone to pick up after and cook for. No, Anne, that's not for me. I'll never love another man."

Anne looked at her sister-in-law, her heart heavy. If anyone needed love it was Rebecca.

Chapter Fifteen

The yeasty smell of rolls and bread permeated the tiny 'front room' store filling Anne's mind with times when there was a baby on one hip and more children playing on the kitchen floor. It was a wonder she hadn't fallen over a child or two as she rushed about the room. Those were good times, the best.

When she closed her eyes she could hear Robert whispering sweet nothings in her ear, as he used to do after capturing her in a bear hug. It's been four years since a man's arms had been about her, and she missed it. She missed the safety circle of being loved and appreciated.

The past eight months preparation for the opening of the Golden Crown Restaurant had been hectic, what with ordering equipment, checking suppliers, setting up a bookkeeping system, making sure the ovens work properly, hiring help, deciding on menus, setting up schedules, buying food, getting fliers printed and ads ready and then rechecking it all again.

School was closed for the summer, and today was the Congregational church picnic, to be held at Josh Reynold's new park, right on the river. The rowboats had been tested and found seaworthy; the river could get nasty if a high wind or rain came up. Even the Catholics were helping set up picnic tables and benches, placing wooden horses and planks for table tops and narrower planks for benches.

Anne's two boys, Robert Jr. and Hugh had been gathering

firewood, filling the shed with ice, salt, apple cider, hot dogs and ice cream churns. No one in Uxbridge had tasted ice cream or hot dogs. There were going to be a great many "maiden voyages" at this year's picnic. A lump formed in her throat when she thought of Robert and how proud he'd be of his handsome sons.

She pulled the high four-legged stool away from the counter, setting it close to the wall behind her, leaned back in the seat and closed her eyes, content to be alone. The leftover hum of people had died, the room was quiet, it would be so easy to fall asleep.

They'd been busy, the bakery full of people, everyone excited and talking at once wondering who was going to the picnic, who had tasted the new foods, and what new outfits the ladies would be wearing. By the time the customer came to order they'd forgotten how many rolls, what kind of bread or what flavor cookies to bring home.

Anne closed her eyes hoping to doze, but her mind was a bottleneck of ideas. Why couldn't they sell ice cream in the bakery, she wondered, put the ice cream in those funny looking cones and they wouldn't have to bother with dishes or spoons. How long did it take to churn a tub of ice cream, how much did one churn hold, how long did the ice last, and how much salt was needed? At five cents a cone it could be a money maker. She'd ask Josh when he came to the house that evening, before she discussed it with Rebecca. Knowing Rebecca, she'd have the cones and be selling ice cream before sunset, but Anne needed to rest, a week or two at least, now that the restaurant was open and running smoothly.

She reached down and tightened her shoe laces until her feet ached, but aching feet were no match for heavy eyelids. The clock on the wall said eleven-ten. She yawned.

Once again she leaned back on the stool and closed her eyes. As much as she loved her sister-in-law, she was aware of their differences, and wise enough to make those differences work for them. Rebecca thrived on work, while she thrived on family. Work was a means to an end for her; to Rebecca, work was a joy unto itself. There was much to be said for both.

Kathleen was a worry to her mother. The girl was guilty of bad judgment and nothing more. Men turned to each other and whispered when Kathleen walked by, making remarks that would cut her daughter deeper than any lash if she'd heard them. Kathleen was lucky to have Josh. It was a puzzling courtship, he seemed smitten, but there was no way of telling how Kathleen felt. The relationship had been going on over half a year now.

Anne was drifting off when the bell over the door jingled, awakening her with a start. She grabbed the counter to keep from falling off the stool.

"Oh, Josh, I'm that glad it's you. I'd never be able to face the neighbors if they'd found me asleep on the job." She reached down and smoothed her crisp, white apron before her fluttering hands adjusted the bun at the nape of her neck. " I thought you'd be at the picnic ground on a busy day like this."

Anne always thought of one of those giant trees in California whenever she saw Josh, big, solid Josh. His blue-black hair and blue-green eyes were typical Irish. Good teeth, none missing or rotted away. He was vain about his teeth, and she understood that. Many of people in Uxbridge, as elsewhere, had few teeth remaining once they were passed their twenties.

"You're looking well, Anne." He leaned against the counter. His shirt was open at the neck and black hair curled up toward his chin.

"I'm afraid Kathleen's not here, Josh. Everybody's busy with the picnic while I mind the store. Not that I mind, mind you." She laughed at her play on words. "Pull up a chair and sit if you have the time, I've been fighting sleep this past half hour."

He placed a an armless chair behind the counter, next to her. "I'm not here to see Kathleen, Anne. I came because I thought you'd be alone." He paused and studied her face, "I'm here to see you, Anne."

Anne wondered if he was here to ask for Kathleen's hand in marriage. But suppose it was something else, how could she answer when Kathleen never confided in her? She had no way of knowing how her daughter felt, she kept everything inside these days. She looked at Josh, his color was high, skin tight across his cheeks. Maybe they've had a spat, or maybe he'll tell me he won't be calling on Kathleen anymore, she thought. Not that she'd blame the man, as indifferent as Kathleen had been to him. "Oh my. There's nothing wrong is there, Josh?"

Josh fingered the coins in his pants pocket. They made a soft musical sound. "Nothing, Anne, but we must talk."

"Has Kathleen done something to upset you?" Anne had marveled at his patience these past months. She wouldn't be surprised if Kathleen had refused him a good-night kiss. As far as she knew, they'd never held hands. "Kathleen's young, and even with a child she's remained a sweet, innocent girl."

"You really don't know, do you, Anne?" Josh looked directly at her, the lines between his eyes deepened into a scowl.

"What don't I know, Josh?" Once again Anne smoothed her apron and tucked imaginary hair into her bun. What could have happened between them, she wondered.

"Kathleen is a lovely girl and if I had a son I'd want him to be Ian, but it's not Kathleen I want, Anne, it's always been you." He gave her a moment. "I knew you wouldn't have me, knew it from the beginning, because of my age, but I'm not that much younger, fifteen years at most, nothing to worry about. But I'd like to court you proper, not hide behind your daughter's skirt, so to speak." He paused. "I want you for my wife, but that will come later. Once you get used to the idea."

For the second time in the past hour Anne grabbed the counter, afraid she'd fall off the stool. Her back straightened. She was unable to speak. Suddenly, there was a fifty pound weight on her chest. This can't be true, she must be dreaming. She was tired when she sat and must have fallen asleep.

Josh took her hand. "Anne, talk to me, say something. You look like you've seen a ghost "

"How could you do this to me?" Anne whispered, "I don't understand."

"I'll get some water, with ice."

Anne listened as Josh fumbled in the kitchen, but she made no move to get off the stool, unsure her legs would hold her. How could this have happened and she be so unaware? Was she the only one who didn't know? Why hadn't someone said something to her? She stared at the clock, not seeing the time, hardly aware where she was.

Josh handed her the glass of water. She held it in her hand a moment before wiping her face with her damp palm. It was cool and felt good against her skin. "Thank you, Josh." She took a long, slow drink. "I don't know what to say." She sipped the water and ran her tongue over the chunk of ice. "How can I talk when I can't think?" She stared at the moist glass. She placed the glass against her cheek.

"Anne, I don't expect an answer today, or next week, but it's time this was out in the open. I can't live with it any longer." His hand went back in his pocket and Anne heard the faint tinkle of coins once again. "If there'd been another way to tell you I would have, but I want you to know I've always loved you, that will never change. Please give me a chance, don't say no, don't be angry. You don't know how I've longed to tell you. To hold your hand, to touch you… please give me a chance. I thought of a hundred ways of telling you so you wouldn't be upset, but telling you straight out seemed the best. It's not fair to me or you, and it's not fair to Kathleen."

They looked up as the bell announced Mrs. Whitehead. "Good morning to you both. You must be the only ones not getting ready."

"You're wrong, Mrs. Whitehead, that's exactly what I've been doing." Josh smiled.

Chapter Sixteen

"Rebecca, we've got to talk.where nobody can hear."

"I'll be finished in a minute," Rebecca reached across the picnic table with a damp rag and swept watermelon seeds to the ground. She'd noticed the lines framing her sister-in-laws eyes and mouth. They hadn't had a chance to talk since arriving at Reynolds Park; they'd been too busy setting up tables, unloading food and keeping track of children.

Anne's skin was as white as the pearls in her ears, her voice as taut as a violin string. Anne shook out her damp rag and flattened it on the table top to dry. "I'd have come to the farm last night but for the thunderstorm, couldn't see my hand in front of my face." She grinned. "Not a fit night for man nor beast, as my mother used to say."

Rebecca pointed to a weeping willow at the edge of the river. "Let's take the blanket nearer the water." She rested her arm across her sister-in-law's shoulders. "You're alright aren't you, not sick or anything?"

"No, no, my head feels like an empty balloon is all." She gave Rebecca a wan smile. "You'll not believe what's happened."

"From the look of you I'd say it wasn't good." Rebecca gave Anne a hug.

"Rebecca, please listen and you'd best not laugh," Anne gazed toward the river and sighed, "No, it's no laughing matter. I just wish it hadn't happened and I'm sure you'll agree."

Three little girls dashed past, pigtails flying as they raced toward the dock. Boats on the river were filled with young people laughing and enjoying themselves. Far from the crowd, Kathleen sat alone at one of the picnic benches, Ian asleep in her lap.

What could possibly have happened? The children were all here, healthy, happy and noisy. Of course, it was hard to tell about Kathleen, she kept so much inside, but she had been happier this past year since Josh had come courting.

Could something be wrong at the bakery or the restaurant, someone quit, an accident of some kind? No, it's more serious than that, but if it's not the children or the business what in the world is it?

They spread the blanket on the soft grass. Anne began talking before she had a chance to sit.

"Anne, Anne, slow down, I can't make head or tail of what you're saying. Start again. It's to do with Josh and the bakery, but it makes no sense."

"I don't know what to do, Becky," Anne mumbled. Clinking horseshoes hitting metal pins echoed through the park followed by the raucous voices of men at play.

Anne leaned back. "I can't talk fast enough, the words keep tripping my tongue." She took a deep breath, adjusted her skirt and checked for loose hairs in her bun. "I tended the bakery yesterday as everyone was helping with the picnic." She cleared her throat. "After things calmed down and I had a chance to sit, Josh came in. I was that surprised to see him, what with the picnic and all, even if it is just across the common. I guess I thought he'd be so busy he'd not get a chance to sit the whole day." She wagged her head in disbelief. "If anyone had told me what he was about to say I'd not have believed a word." Anne's hands continued to flutter to the bun on the back of her neck; graceful butterflies flirting with a rose.

Rebecca listened, expecting Josh had found someone new and wouldn't be calling on Kathleen again; something along that line; instead she was left stunned as Anne told her of Josh's proposal of marriage. Was it possible Anne had misconstrued what Josh had to say? Why had he waited so long to tell her? How deeply involved was he with Kathleen? Had he made her any promises? So many questions. Rebecca sat, deep in thought. She wasn't aware Anne had stopped talking until she heard, "You're as dumb struck as me, it's written all over you." Anne flicked a large black ant off the blanket. "I've got to ask, though I'm sure you didn't, did you know anything of this or suspect it?"

"The last thing I'd have ever thought." Hoping to ease the tension she added, "It's hard to imagine anyone wanting an old lady of forty, isn't it?" Rebecca watched as tears filled her sister-in-laws eyes. "I shouldn't be teasing. I'm that sorry, it hurts to see you like this." She reached over for her hand and held it. "Have you spoken with Kathleen?"

"Not a word, I had to talk with you first. I was hoping she'd said something to you, told you how she feels about Josh." Tears started down her cheeks, "She's always been able to talk easier with you than me. Maybe that's the way of it between mother and daughter."

The voices of children playing near the dock and men laughing and roughhousing at the horseshoe pits went unheard as the two women sat, a dazed look upon their faces. The fires for cooking had been extinguished but smoke lingered in the air, a friendly comfortable fragrance. " I can't imagine how you felt. " She leaned back and rested her elbows on the blanket. "No, Kathleen's not said a word to me. You know how she is, she'll tell everything when she's ready and not before." Rebecca looked at Anne. "Maybe it's the wrong time, but I've got to ask, do you have any feelings for Josh?"

Anne gazed into the distance. "Where Kathleen's concerned, yes, he's been courting my daughter for over six months so I'm certainly interested in him." She didn't expect a response. "I don't plan to marry again, me with four children at home, not counting Kathleen and the baby. Where would I get the time? I don't get to bed till after midnight what with the bookkeeping and all the other things we have to do. You know only too well what I mean. We're both so busy it's a wonder we have time to sleep and what man would want to burden himself with a ready-made family?" Once more, she gave Rebecca no time to answer. "It's an awful thing to find your love wants someone else, and when the someone else turns out to be your mother it's beyond hurt. Kathleen will feel she's been slashed to death. I hope she feels nothing but friendship for Josh or her heart will be broken twice, poor child." Anne stood and started back to the table for a bottle of ginger beer, but Rebecca stopped her. "Sit, I'll get it."

Rebecca handed the open bottle to Anne as Anne continued to speculate. " She's afraid of getting hurt again that's why she's put so much space between them. It must be that, what else could it be?" Boats began returning to the dock as the sun disappeared behind an ugly gray cloud. "Or some reason we don't know, but how can he resist a young girl as lovely as Kathleen! He's told me he loves Ian like a son, so half the battle's won."

Rebecca marveled at Anne, who was unaware how attractive she was. Josh Reynolds was determined to have her, that was obvious. Hadn't the man been calling at the house for over half a year! Anyone else would have given up long ago, and here Anne was talking as if she could convince Josh he loved Kathleen .

"When are you going to talk to Kathleen?" Rebecca asked.

"As soon as possible. It'll be an awful blow to her." Anne flicked another ant off the blanket. "Poor child has had enough without this."

"Would it help if I was with you?" Rebecca waited, sure of the answer. "She's got to be told ...without crushing her completely."

Anne interrupted. "Other than Ian, all Kathleen has left is her pride." Anne's eyes brimmed with tears as she looked at Rebecca. "You know how grateful I'd be to have you there. Poor child."

"After the children are put to bed." Rebecca looked out toward the river.

The sun broke through the clouds and most of the boats returned to deeper water. "It might be best to feel her out a bit before you say anything." Rebecca looked at Anne, unable to smile. "This day's been full of surprises I wish I didn't know."

"My nerves are standing up like the hairs on the back of a

Halloween cat." Anne squeezed her hands together and closed her eyes in silent prayer as she added, "Oh, what a crazy world we live in."

Chapter Seventeen

How to tell Kathleen, whose life had been anything but happy these past five years? Being a divorcée, gossip swirled about her head like leaves in an October windstorm and now she had this additional blow to her pride.

Rebecca and Anne sat across from one another at the kitchen table. Rebecca's teacup was clutched tight in her hand. Anne was counting threads in the red and white checked tablecloth. Her pallor was the gray it got whenever she was upset. Kathleen was upstairs seeing to the children; she would be down in a few minutes.

There could be no happy ending to this affair. If mother and daughter remained friends or even speaking it would be a miracle. Kathleen would never understand, never realize how overwhelmed and upset her mother had been, Kathleen wouldn't be able to see beyond her own pride. Why didn't Josh tell Anne in the beginning? No, he was right, she would have told him to find someone his own age, more suitable, and Josh wouldn't have been allowed to call at the house again.

Kathleen was coming down the stairs. Rebecca poured tea in Kathleen's cup and set the sugar bowl next to it. She didn't take cream so Rebecca left the pitcher where it was. Anne hadn't said a word. Why was her daughter always on the brink of breaking with her family, first for a man she loved and now for a man she probably didn't love, one who could cause a breach so wide mother and daughter would be unable to reach each other.

Kathleen collapsed into the chair next to Rebecca. "Ian's asleep. Without a nap he was so sleepy I almost didn't put him in the tub." She stirred sugar into her cup. "All the children are asleep and you two look as if you should join them."

Rebecca and Anne sat in their chairs, shuffling their feet and shifting from one hip to another. Anne's eyes were puffy and red as, if she'd been crying. She picked up her cup and took her fifth sip. Neither woman could look Kathleen in the eye

"What's the matter, don't you feel well? Have I done something wrong?" The overhead lamp illuminated the table like a boxing ring, each contestant sitting statue like in her own corner. The remainder of the room was in deep shadow.

"Of course not," Anne mumbled.

"Then why are we sitting here like statues?"

Rebecca waited but Anne said nothing, "It's about Josh Reynolds. Your mother has something to tell you."

Kathleen covered her mouth with her hand as color drained from her face. "Is he alright, is he sick or something?"

Rebecca waited, but Anne remained mute. It was impossible to tell if she'd heard. "No, he's fine. Yesterday he had a talk with your mother." Rebecca paused, hoping Anne would finish but Anne continued to stare at her hands and say nothing. " It's about the two of you." Rebecca added. If only Anne would talk...

"He hasn't asked for my hand, has he?" Rebecca heard dismay in Kathleen's voice. Because Josh asked or because he'd waited so long to ask? Rebecca didn't have long to wonder.

Anne reached across the table for her daughter's hand. "No, darling, he told me he won't be courting you any longer. You don't seem interested in him."

"I like Josh, but I'm not in love with him, and I can't make myself love somebody I don't. I wish I could but I can't." Her eyes flooded with tears as she added, "I know I should have told him. I've wanted to tell him for a long time, but if I did everybody would be laughing because I didn't have a beau. It's bad enough being divorced without that." She made her fingers into steeples as she looked up at the two women. "Being divorced in Uxbridge is bad enough, but..." her voice trailed off.

"Nobody's laughing at you. Running away to get married is nothing to be ashamed of, and you're not the only divorced woman in the state, you know," Anne couldn't refrain from protecting this cherished child, if only for a moment, "but you can't keep a man waiting forever. Josh has been very patient with you, it's a wonder he's waited this long."

"You've got to tell Kathleen the rest, Anne." Rebecca knew how difficult it was going to be. She'd have been as frozen as her sister-in-law if this were happening between her and Roseanna. Telling your daughter something that could put an end to your loving relationship was beyond imagining.

Anne poured more tea in her cup. Her hand was shaking but color was returning to her face and her voice sounded normal. Rebecca waited for her to continue, to tell Kathleen that Josh wanted to marry her, but Anne was silent. Anne patted her daughter's hand. "Kathleen, I don't know how to tell you this and make you understand, but you must remember I knew nothing of this before yesterday. It was the biggest surprise of my life. Josh had told me he wants to marry me...and I'm not over it yet."

The pregnant silence was broken when Kathleen began to speak in a low monotone, every word carefully enunciated. "You've made a fool of me, all of you, you and him. Everybody will get a big laugh out of this. My husband runs off with another woman and now my beau wants to marry my mother." She glared at her mother, her voice no longer low. "Did you encourage him? Were you laughing behind my back the whole time?" She jumped up, banging her hip against the table. Her chair careened across the linoleum and crashed to the floor behind her. "How could you do this to me! I'll not stay in the same house with you. You disgust me, pretending to love me and all the time sneaking behind my back. You must feel very proud of yourself for what you've done, you and him!"

Rebecca put an arm across her niece's shoulder. "Stop, Kathleen. You come to the farm with me tonight, until you get control of yourself. I'll bring Ian out in the morning if that's what you want."

Kathleen tried to interrupt but Rebecca stopped her. "You've said enough, say no more. Once it's said it's forever alive. There's no way of unsaying it." She held Kathleen.

"You know your mother loves you, and would never hurt you. She's as stunned as you. No one ever set out to hurt you. You must remember that."

"Fine." She shook herself free and started for the door. "I'll be back for Ian in the morning."

"Oh, Kathleen, I'd never harm a hair on your head." Anne looked up at her daughter, unable to stop the tears. "I knew nothing of this. Why would I do such a thing? Never. You've got to believe me."

Kathleen turned and looked at her mother, her eyes hard and mouth unsmiling. " I don't care what you have to say, I never want to see you again...ever."

Chapter Eighteen

Kathleen hadn't been to the farm for the joint birthday parties for two years, but yesterday when Rebecca went to her apartment, Kathleen broke down and cried. It was the first sign of remorse since she told her mother she never wanted to see her again. She had said she'd like to end the rift but couldn't bring herself to go to her mother's house. "Would my mother come here, do you think?"

"And have the door slammed in her face again? Not likely, twice was more than enough. It's up to you, Kathleen." Rebecca sat on the edge of the chair. "Your mother loves you, heaven knows why, you've given her enough grief. Her happiest day will come when you're seated at her kitchen table, a hot cup of tea in hand."

That was how it was left. They'd have to wait and see.

Rebecca stretched her arms above her head, pulled the sheet up under her chin, yawned and settled back in bed. Downstairs she could hear Mary banging pots and pans in the kitchen, getting ready for the party. Eating one of Mary's cakes was like tasting Van Gogh's "Sunflowers" or a Monet lily. Rebecca couldn't suppress a grin. How could anyone make so much noise icing a cake? she wondered.

How nice it would be if Emma stayed home this year and just sent her two little girls! But that would never happen, not with Emma, the more uncomfortable she made everyone the happier she was, particularly if that someone was Rebecca, but her girls always had such a good time it would be a shame to deprive them if they weren't invited.

Rebecca stared up at the ceiling. This coming week would be a busy one. Monday to Boston to see Richard Drummond. Richard handled all the legal affairs for the Rebecca-Anne Bakeries and the Golden Crown restaurant. He'd been their lawyer since the business first opened, back when his office was in Uxbridge. They'd stayed with him despite his move to Boston and she was glad in view of all that had happened.

Richard was an attractive man — not handsome but attractive. He had a Huck Finn look about him and a dry sense of humor, which he used often. He hummed when he danced. It was like dancing with Rudolph Valentino or some other romantic movie star. He was hard to describe, other than to say he had a friendly, trustworthy face. Good attributes for a lawyer.

He wouldn't have offered her a buggy ride to the hotel that memorable afternoon if the snow hadn't been so thick she couldn't see the tips of her toes. He denied this, saying he'd wanted to ask her to dinner for ages but was afraid she'd refuse.

The dining room tables in the Copley dining room were covered with white linen cloths, the place settings were English china, the food excellent . Rebecca was surprised the first time it happened but she'd learned to wait for the waiter put the napkin in her lap. The deep blue carpeting and velvet drapes created an impressive elegance, conducive to intimacy.

Being alone in a restaurant with a man felt odd after so many years, but she was soon talking about David, Roseanna and the rest of her family and he told her how he'd met his wife and how anxious they were to have their first child, never dreaming she'd be dead a few hours after the baby was born.

The candle flickered and died, drowning in its own wax before they looked up and realized they were alone. It was four hours since they had ordered and eaten. The lobby was quiet except for the night clerk, hidden behind a quivering newspaper, snoring so loud the ashtrays danced on the counter. When they said goodnight at the elevator Richard held her hand longer than necessary. She didn't pull away.

Rebecca thought of Hester Prynne, wearer of the infamous letter "A," a woman well remembered in Massachusetts. Unmarried women engaging in sex were shunned by friends, family and neighbors. There was no one who would speak to her; but Rebecca didn't plan on being Hester Prynne

As more time passed Rebecca knew she should break off this affair with Richard. If Roseanna found out she'd despise her. She and Anne could lose everything, but how could she give Richard up when he made the emptiness disappear? No longer was she a half person. Every meeting made her feel like a child seeing her first Christmas tree. When they were apart she longed to be with him. Her life had become all memories and wanting to hear his voice and feel his touch.

She'd never been this close to anyone before. Sex with Richard was relaxed, more relaxed than with David. She wasn't sure why. That didn't mean she admitted she enjoyed sex, because she couldn't; her upbringing wouldn't allow it.

It was unlikely she'd get pregnant at her age, so how was anyone to know? she wondered.

Laughter drifted up from the kitchen. I've got to get out of bed and help Mary, she told herself. I so hope Kathleen comes today. What a wonderful surprise it would be for Anne.

She sat on the edge of the bed and slipped her feet into her slippers before starting down the hall to the bathroom. Despite the day ahead her mind continued to linger in the past.

Rebecca knew Anne would accept Josh if she and Kathleen were at peace. Not that Anne had said so, but it was obvious when they were together. There was a great deal of love between them and the children adored Josh. It wasn't as if Kathleen's heart was broken. Her pride had been bruised, but the discoloration faded long ago; it was the nurturing she enjoyed.

Josh Reynolds Park now had a sand hill and swings for the children, three more rowboats and a half dozen canoes tied up at the second dock, and bicycles to rent. Josh had Chuck Warner to manage for him as the lumberyard took up most of his time now, but he never missed an evening with Anne. Often in the lingering light of summer, he took Anne and the children, Ian included, for a row on the river. Ian spent a lot of time at his grandmother's house. That's one nice thing Kathleen did, allow Ian and his grandmother time together.

Rebecca returned to the bedroom washed and clean, ready to dress. She heard Roseanna laughing down stairs, probably at something Mary said. Oh, let it be a good birthday for Anne, let Kathleen come so they can celebrate their joint birthdays, let us all be happy again. Rebecca thought often of her loving relationship with Roseanna, so different from Kathleen and Anne. She prayed it never changed.

Her daughter Roseanna was tumbling between childhood and being a young lady. She was not as beautiful as Kathleen. Her sand colored hair and light blue eyes were the color of David's. Whenever Roseanna smiled or talked two enchanting dimples skittered in and out of her cheeks. She was more outgoing than Kathleen, a lot like her mother in that respect and popular with boys, a born flirt, unwilling or unable to settle on one boy.

A houseful of company coming in a few hours and here she was dreaming when she should be helping in the kitchen, Rebecca chided herself. Maybe Grant Logan will stop by. Said he would try and join them after the baseball game this afternoon.

Grant had managed the restaurant these past few months. It was Anne who insisted on hiring him and she was right, it had given them both more time and freedom. His name was Burton Grant Logan. He said his family called him 'BG' but he'd appreciate it if they all called him 'Grant,' it sounded more like a man than a kid. He was twenty-four years old, from a small town somewhere in Virginia.

Rebecca had no idea what an important part he'd play in her life.

Chapter Nineteen

Picnics required a lot of work. Rebecca picked up the Windsor chair and headed for the kitchen door. She took a few steps on the recently mowed lawn and set the chair down. It was lovely out, much too nice to go inside. She took a deep breath. The only thing that smelled better than fresh cut grass was a baby bathed, powdered and ready for bed. She watched as the garden nodded and yawned, the afternoon shadows were beginning to blanket the bold reds and greens.

A breeze, so lazy it couldn't turn a leaf, caressed her arms. The high-colored vegetables, tomatoes, eggplant, and radishes had mellowed in the afternoon light . Overgrown strawberry vines wriggled their way over moss covered rocks in search of the garden path. Corn silk shone as golden as the head of a two-year-old. The delicate yellow and white squash blossoms were gone, replaced by bright orange, yellow and green vegetables. Plump tomatoes, shiny red in snug little green caps peeked flirtatiously from beneath lacy leaves. Rebecca cradled a tomato in her hand. She didn't pick it, just held it. It smelled of earth and was as warm as an egg snatched from under a sitting hen. Rebecca's favorite fruit was within reach, but without sugar the cultivated strawberries were not as tasty as their smaller, wilder cousins who made up with sweetness what they lacked in size.

Rebecca sat on the bench in the herb garden. Cheese, one of many cats of the same name, was asleep on a flat granite rock in the middle of the herbs. It may not have been soft but it was warm.

Rebecca sniffed the mint leaf she'd snapped in two. So cool and clean smelling. She ran her finger across a saucer-shaped gourd. It felt as smooth as corn starch. Come fall, the inside would dry, turning it into a giant castanet. Lethargic pumpkins would soon emerge from beneath their large green leaves.

Rebecca looked past the horse barns to the fields where the horses grazed, heads down, tails giving an occasional flick. They were forever nudging or leaning against each other whispering.

She could hear but could not see the Mumford river. Rebecca closed her eyes. At first morning frost, the Mumford disappeared, hidden beneath a downy mist of fog, but at this time of year it was clear, bright, playful and eager. Mozart rhythms lured the dreamer to the river's edge in spring while Strauss filled the hot summer days. The rushing water picked up the thundering horns and drums of Beethoven with the coming of winter.

Her thoughts drifted back to the early part of the day. Kathleen hadn't come, but that wasn't surprising, and of course, Emma had. That wasn't surprising either. Emma was her usual self, just this side of surly. Rebecca always found herself looking over her shoulder and whispering when Emma was there. How was she able to make everyone feel her presence in such a malignant way?

Emma's eyebrows rose and she'd smirked when Anne and Rebecca talked about Rebecca's trip to Boston on Monday. "Going to Boston a lot these days aren't you, Rebecca?"

Like it was any of her business.

Emma marched out, letting the screen door slam behind her.

Rebecca had chairs to return to the kitchen. She'd not leave Anne to do all the work. She walked back to the house, reluctant to leave the sounds and smells of her yard. She looked across the yard and saw Grant and Roseanna sitting on the grass. Why were they sitting so close, and why was Roseanna blushing? It wasn't like her.

Chapter Twenty

Roseanna had watched as Grant walked down the road toward her house, twirling his baseball cap and whistling, It was the day of the joint birthday parties which were more like a wake because Kathleen never came. She might as well be dead, she'd put so much distance between herself and the rest of the family.

Roseanna couldn't take her eyes away from Grant.

She stayed hidden behind the lilac bush on the front porch Her chest was heavy, making it hard to breathe and there was a warm feeling between her thighs. She didn't know the word lust. Fifteen-year-old girls didn't know what sex was, much less lust. It was a good thing she was alone, she'd been looking at him as if he was chocolate cake covered with cherries and whipped cream.

When he got closer she saw his eyes were the color of the Mumford river on a spring morning, when you could count the rocks and pebbles on the sandy bottom. Clear green.

All five-feet-two of Roseanna reached as high as Grant's adam's apple; he was that tall, six feet or more, she discovered later. He kept pushing his thick brown, wavy hair out of his eyes, but it was a waste of time as it fell right back down again. When he stood it was like he was on third base waiting to steal home.

He had this wonderful way of talking, slow and easy, not like Uxbridge people. When he looked at her, he saw her. Not like he was about to pat her on the head or give her a scratch behind the ears. She was an adult to him. She could see it in his eyes.

Roseanna stammered something when they were introduced; she couldn't remember what but nobody seemed to notice. She looked around the kitchen as if she'd never been here before, but she knew nothing had changed. Her mother and Aunt Anne were cleaning up leftover food, scraping dishes and putting away rolls. Emma stood, her back stiff like it always was around Rebecca, running hot water in the sink. Children were scooting in and out, under the table and out the back door. The round oak table in the middle of the room was covered with dishes waiting to be washed, but somehow everything was different. The children's voices were softer and sweeter, Aunt Anne was prettier, her mother looked younger, the birthday cakes more mouth-watering. Everything had changed since Grant arrived, yet it remained the same.

"Take Grant out and show him around the farm, Roseanna."

When Grant put his hand on her elbow, her knees buckled. Could she be coming down with something, maybe have a temperature? She leaned toward him, wishing his arm was around her waist not on her elbow. Her temperature must be very high.

She stole a quick glance at his face. He smiled down at her. Her heart turned to feathers and fluttered around in her chest.

"Come, Roseanna, show me your farm," he said. She didn't reply because she couldn't find her voice.

She wasn't sure what Grant was feeling, but whatever it was she knew her mother wouldn't approve. She could hear her now. "We don't know his family, don't know anything about him. There are many nice younger boys here in Uxbridge." Roseanna didn't care who or what his family was, but Momma would.

Roseanna was planning on going to school in Boston to study art in September, and until this afternoon that was exactly what Roseanna wanted, but not any more. She'd be content to help in the bakeries or the restaurant as long as she could be near Grant.

She kept her head down, afraid to look up, afraid her mother would see her face and read her thoughts.

They walked out the back door toward the barns, where the boarding horses were kept.

"Do you like living on a farm, Roseanna?" Grant took her by the hand.

"I've never lived any place else," she explained. "I was born in Missouri but I don't remember it." She felt the calluses in his palm. From playing baseball, probably. She knew she should remove her hand, but it felt good, even if his hand was all sweaty.

Grant told her he loved her and he was going to marry her. She was addled, unable to believe what she'd heard. Could she be making it up because that's what she wanted to hear? Her mind was so noisy it was hard to think.

She couldn't believe Grant. He had to be teasing her, as if she were a child. For once in her life her mouth stayed shut, she didn't know what to say. Here she was thrilled just to be holding hands, and he was talking marriage. Momma was really going to be mad.

Roseanna knew this without giving it a second thought.

Chapter Twenty-one

"Get in the house this minute, Roseanna! And you, Grant Logan, get off this property and never set foot here or in the restaurant again. Get out and stay out." Rebecca turned to Roseanna, "I've paced the floor all night, not knowing where you were." Despite her order to Roseanna, Rebecca continued to block the kitchen door. The three of them glared at each other. Tears filled Rebecca's eyes but only for an instant. She straightened her back. With a shrug she stepped back and held the door open keeping her arm ready to block the entrance in case Grant tried to enter the house.

"Not you. just Roseanna."

Roseanna continued to hold Grant's hand. "If Grant can't come in, I'm not welcome either." Roseanna was pale but there was no mistaking the determined set of her chin. Rebecca knew that look well, she'd displayed it many times herself.

Anne's words from last night ran through her mind: don't do anything to alienate Roseanna, you don't want a situation like I have with Kathleen. Listen to what she has to say. If Grant's with her, remember he could be your son-in-law one day, the father of your grandchildren. Think, Rebecca, think before you speak.

So far she'd not heeded a word.

There was so much of David in Roseanna, so much love and tenderness. The simplest things pleased her. It would be impossible for Rebecca to go through life without the unexpected hugs or touch of her daughter's hand. She couldn't lose Roseanna but what could she do about this man, this Grant Logan? Would he treat her daughter with the love she deserved, would he be kind and affectionate? Would he be gentle? After all, what did they know about him, other than he said he was from Virginia?

Rebecca loved Richard, but not with the same love she felt for her daughter. Love varied; some times it was as sweet as a rose while at other times it was a vine of nettles. Again she could hear Anne's voice: you'll love her more than anyone...that's what Anne had said that cold winter day she walked to her brother's house, carrying the child inside her, to ask for help

Rebecca stepped back. "Come in, where we can talk." *Now, that's better*, Rebecca told herself, more like Anne advised.

She waited while Grant pulled a chair around until he was sitting next to Roseanna at the round table. No one spoke, they looked at each other like the gingham dog and the calico cat. Rebecca knew the poem ended with bits and pieces of gingham and calico flying about the room, but there would be no pulling apart of her family, Rebecca thought to herself, not by this young man or anyone else.

The farm kitchen had changed since that March day when she and Anne first unpacked. A chandelier now hung above the table. It had four frosted globes trimmed with yellow and blue flowers. More appropriate for the front parlor, Anne had said, but Rebecca didn't care, she liked it and that's where she wanted it.

She hoped Roseanna and Grant couldn't hear the pugnacious thundering in her chest. Rebecca filled the teakettle and placed a cup and saucer in front of each of them. What happened next would not be pleasant. Her skin felt flushed and her ears whined with the stillness.

"You could have talked to me before running off with Grant."

"It wouldn't have done any good, you'd have had a fit." Roseanna traced a design on the tablecloth with the handle of her teaspoon. She didn't look up.

"What about you, Grant? Roseanna's reputation is ruined,

maybe her life, yet neither of you had the decency to talk to me." Rebecca's voice cracked. She cleared her throat. "Why?" The teakettle whistled. Rebecca turned off the gas and poured boiling water into the waiting teapot.

"It's not like you think, Mrs. Hawley." Grant pushed his hair out of his eyes. "You love Roseanna and so do I, but you'd never have let us go." He shifted in his chair. "You'd have made us wait."

"She'll be eighteen in two months. Is that too much to ask? "

"But, Momma, we had to get married, we just had to." Roseanna set the teaspoon in the saucer and for the first time looked her mother in the eye.

"Then you're pregnant?"

"No, Mrs. Hawley, Roseanna's not pregnant." Grant reached over and laid his hand atop Roseanna's hand.

"Would you be kind enough to tell me what's going on? " The cup clipped the edge of the saucer but made no chip. Relief at having her daughter home overwhelmed her and tears started down her cheeks. "I always wanted you to have a big wedding, flowers, bridesmaids, a maid of honor." She dabbed at her eyes with the back of her hand. "Why didn't you say something?"

"Because you'd have said no. You'd have told us to wait, and we didn't want to wait. We've waited three years already."

"I'm sorry Mrs. Hawley."

Rebecca stared into her cup. The tea was tepid and she still hadn't taken a sip. She continued to stir. "Not being pregnant is a blessing." She squeezed her daughter's hand. "At least for now." Roseanna and Grant's hands were clasp tight together. They were sitting so close their bodies almost touched.

"You know, of course, if it hadn't been for Anne telling me to let Roseanna have a little more freedom, I'd never have let you court my daughter, not that I'm blaming this on Anne. Or anyone but myself for that matter."

"We'd have met without you knowing it, Momma. I loved Grant the first time I saw him" Roseanna smiled at the memory. "You remember when he came to the Fourth of July picnic and you asked me to show him around the farm, well, he asked me to marry him then."

"It goes that far back?" Rebecca was stunned, "I knew you were attracted to each other, but you were so young, Roseanna, and I credited Grant with having more sense." Rebecca set her cup down. "Roseanna, you'll not be able to go to school in Boston, not now. There's no school will take a married woman."

"I know that, but what I want is to be with Grant, not to go to school."

How well I remember that feeling, Rebecca thought, David's arms around me and me wanting to stay there forever. She pushed the memory to the back of her mind. Now I have a daughter with the same passionate nature as myself. God help her.

She looked at the young people, the two of them sitting like children waiting for the wagon to take them for a hayride. There was no way she could have stopped it. At least there wasn't a child on the way. She sighed with relief. Why can no one in this family marry in the usual way, in a nice church ceremony? she wondered. She was jolted from her thoughts,

"Momma, we've got something else to tell you." Roseanna's eye brows were drawn into a frown.

"There's nothing more you can say to upset me." Rebecca sighed.

Roseanna hesitated, the words refuse to come. Grant said, "We're married, but not really."

"What do you mean you're not really married; you ran away together but you aren't married? What does that mean?" Rebecca's mind spun in all directions as she searched for an answer

"Mrs. Hawley, I love Roseanna. I'll always love Roseanna, but I already have a wife." He dropped his eyes, unable to meet Rebecca's scorching glare. Rebecca's face was as white as the sugar in the bowl in front of her.

"And where is your wife, if I may ask?" Ice coated every word.

"In Virginia. Back home. We haven't seen each other in over three years, and I won't see her ever again."

"I'm afraid to ask, but are there any children?"

"No, no, there aren't." Grant cleared his throat. "I'd marry Roseanna in a second if I was free, but being a Roman Catholic that's impossible for…a…Harriet," he fumbled over the name "my wife, will never give me a divorce."

Roseanna poured fresh tea. "It's not really as bad as you think, Momma."

"Don't tell me what I think," Rebecca snapped.

Roseanna continued as if her mother hadn't spoken."Nobody in Uxbridge will ever find out. We took the train to New York City and then to New Jersey and got married in Newark. We used our middle names, and said we were from Troy, New York." Roseanna put the cozy on the teapot ."Nobody will ever know unless you tell them."

"You know, of course, you're committing bigamy. You can go to jail." Rebecca glared at the two of them, her heart breaking and now this. Grant married with a wife. "That not only puts an end to art school, it puts an end to everything."

"I don't want to go to art school. I want to stay with Grant." Roseanna tried to smile. "Nobody will know, Momma. There's no way they can find out. If you say we got married everybody will believe you. Please, Momma, do this for me." Roseanna begged her mother. "Wouldn't you have run away with Papa if this had happened to you?"

Rebecca eyes softened as she looked at her daughter. "I loved your father, Roseanna, but I can't say what I would have done. It was a long time ago and…"

"Do you think you'll be called up to serve in the army? Rebecca suddenly turned to Grant. "The war looking as bad as it does?" Rebecca saw the stricken look on Roseanna's face and her heart ached.

"I'd like to go and fight for my country."

"And leave a wife and possible a child here, alone. Are you sure your wife won't change her mind? Have you asked her?" Rebecca watched Grant closely, hoping she wouldn't see signs of deceit.

"She'll bite off her nose to spite her face. It's the last thing she'd ever do, give me my freedom."

"She may have found someone by now and is waiting to hear from you."

"She'll never find anyone. She'll be happy to spend the rest of her life making my life as miserable as she can." He spat out the last sentence. "No, Mrs. Hawley, Harriet won't give me a divorce, I can assure you of that."

"Can you get something from the church that will free you?"

"A papal dispensation? Hardly. I'm not Catholic, so I don't need one, and there's no reason for the church to give her one." His arm was around the back of Roseanna's chair. "Mrs. Hawley, I'll sign any paper you want, anything. That I'll take care of Roseanna the rest of my life, anything you can think of, as long as you give us the chance to be together for the rest of our lives."

Rebecca had hoped it was puppy love and would pass, that she'd get interested in one of the young Uxbridge men, but it never happened. It was always Grant.

"It doesn't look as if I have any choice."

Chapter Twenty-two

"Ladies Home Reader" it said in the left upper corner but the envelope wasn't heavy enough to be the story she'd sent. Kathleen leaned against the kitchen table. The edge cut into her hip as she continued to stare at the letter, hands shaking, clutching the envelope as tight as an abalone clinging to a rock.

A story rejection always made her feel like a child caught in her mother's jewelry box without permission, like she'd done something bad, but the feeling was short-lived. To stop writing was impossible. It would have been easier to stop breathing. Head down, blinders on both eyes, she plodded, polished and perfected her stories, enjoying the scenery along the way, not caring about the bag of oats at the end of the trail.

Moving to the apartment above the bakery had come as an aftermath of the argument with her mother. Kathleen's world had changed, but not as drastically as she'd feared; in retrospect, a feather blade falling on a cotton chopping block. She enjoyed her apartment and having Ian to herself. She was getting to know him as she never would have living at "home" with her family, but she missed her mother, her siblings, the laughter and spats that were part of that life.

Kathleen envied Ian; she longed to be welcome in her mother's home. Every Saturday he walked there by himself, chest pushed out like a barnyard rooster and him only four years old. His grandmother's house was only six houses down the street, but

Kathleen watched him every step of the way.

Maude Miller was the only person in town who might suspect Kathleen was writing again. Maude had worked in the post office as long as anyone could remember. As Postmaster, she sold Kathleen stamps and large envelopes in which to mail her manuscripts. She'd never asked Kathleen what she was mailing. It was none of her business. "Mornin'," "afternoon," or "a-ah" was a lengthy chat with Miss Miller.

So many times Kathleen wished her mother could read what she was writing now, make suggestions, correct the spelling, add a phrase here and there, give her ideas, but how could she ask when they hadn't spoken in more than three years?

Kathleen sighed as she turned the envelope over in her hand. Nothing on the back. Why was she torturing herself like this? Maybe she'd forgotten to sign her name or send return postage. She was cold despite the beads of sweat on her upper lip and the water shivering its way down her spine. Kathleen rested her hand on the back of the Windsor chair as she daydreamed, pretending her story had been accepted, that someone read and liked it. Hope before rejection, hope before she reads why they are returning her story; "We are not accepting stories of this nature. Please read our magazine to get an idea what type stories we are interested in before submitting again," etc..

The story she sent was about Ian and Zipper. Zipper was a mixed-breed dog with a shaggy black goatee, and a happy grin. The pads of his rubbery feet caused him to bounce with every step. His furry black tail acted like a periscope, wagging in all directions. Zipper showed up at the bakery one snowy evening and Ian refused to go to bed until she let him in. Ian liked the sound of the word "zipper" so that's what he named him. That was a year ago.

The chair accepted her weight without so much as a groan. With elbows resting on the red and white checked tablecloth she took the paring knife and slit open the envelope. A folded sheet of paper dropped to the table. She opened it, and a check fell out. She left it where it landed, face down on the tablecloth. She was afraid to look at it, afraid it wasn't a check; more shattered hopes. She picked up the letter: "Dear Mrs. Eaton, Thank you for your story, "A Day in the Life of Ian and Zipper." Enclosed is a check in the amount of $75.00 dollars. Would it be possible to meet with you in our Boston office next Thursday? We have given you a 10:30 appointment with Graham Field, one of our editors. If this is not convenient please let us know. Sincerely," etc.

The check lay atop the table. She was stunned. It was impossible to believe after all those submissions, someone liked her story. She was unable to open the letter, afraid if she read it again the words would have changed, afraid it was figment of her imagination, like one of her stories, but she was unable to stop herself. When she read it again the words were the same.

Kathleen cradled the envelope in her hands and started for her bedroom. She took her purse from the closet shelf, flicked the metal clasp open, and shoved the letter and the check inside.

In her haste she forgot to lock the backdoor. The key could be anywhere, probably in one of the kitchen drawers but no one in Uxbridge locked their door, why should they? Her mother would be so happy to hear the news; Anne was the only one who knew how long and hard she'd worked. In her excitement Kathleen gave no thought to how her mother would greet her.

She clutched her purse in both hands, afraid the letter would fly away or manage to escape. Why was it taking so long to get there, it was just down the street. It hadn't entered her mind that her mother might not be home.

Anne usually worked at the farm office, but this morning she decided to stay at home and had her accounts set up on the kitchen table. She sat facing the back door. Between her and the door dust motes frolicked in the broad swath of sunlight that came through the windows above the sink. She stopped and listened. It sounded as if someone was running down the drive toward the backdoor.

Running footfalls or surprise visits have never brought good news. The boys were in school so it wasn't them, and it couldn't be

Rebecca, she was at the bakery in Worchester today.

Kathleen pushed the backdoor open and for the first few moments didn't see her mother sitting at the table as she rushed into the kitchen. The dog jumped from under the table where he'd been sleeping and barked. Anne reached down and patted his head. "It's alright boy, stay where you are." Anne said nothing to Kathleen as she waited for her to speak. Why was she running as if the devil was a step behind her, unless something had happened to Ian.

She watched, afraid to ask, as Kathleen fumbled with the clasp on her purse, trying to get it open. It was then Anne noticed Kathleen's disheveled appearance; the tail of her light blue blouse hanging out of her skirt, her skirt twisted about her waist. Her belt buckle turned inside out, her blouse buttoned in the wrong holes. Anne stepped back, arms never leaving her sides.

Oh, to be able to hug her, to be safe and warm in her arms, Kathleen thought, can it ever be like that again?

"Kathleen, is something wrong? Is Ian alright?"

"Ian's at Mrs. White's next door, Momma." She paused and looked down at the envelope she was holding, "He's fine."

Why are you here then?" There was neither love nor hate on Anne's face, just a wary waiting to hear what her daughter had to say. She made no move to sit, or offer her daughter a chair.

"Please read this letter." Kathleen placed the "Ladies Home Reader " envelope in her hand. "I want you so much to read it. Please"

Anne removed the letter and the check. She set the check on the table without looking at it, and opened the sheet of paper. Kathleen watched her mother read, looking for signs of pleasure on her face. There were none.

When finished she said, "Congratulations Kathleen, I'm happy for you and I'm sure you're more then pleased." She folded the letter, inserted the check and handed them to her.

Kathleen didn't realize she was crying until her mother put a handkerchief in her hand." Oh, Momma, please don't be like this. I want to share this with you, I thought you'd be excited for me."

"I'm excited for you, Kathleen, but what makes you think you can come into my home as if nothing has happened and expect me to welcome you with open arms? You've done too much damage to the family as it is." Anne turned her back and walked around the table to her chair. Laying her hand on the table, she lowered herself into the chair. She looked old, old and tired. "Who knows what you'll do next. I haven't the time for your pouting tantrums. Your father always said I spoiled you and he was right." She looked up at Kathleen, "I hope someday you'll outgrow it and be a decent human being. I'll always love you, but I don't like you, don't like what you've become — self-centered, someone who cares little who she tramples as long as she gets her own way. I hope, for your sake, there have been moments when you've had regrets and wished for a second chance.

"I'm unsure how Josh feels about you. You're not a big topic of conversation in this house. You've done damage that can never be repaired all for the sake of your willful pride." Anne watched her daughter's face change to a mottled white. "Has it been worth it to you?"

"Momma, I'm glad you and Josh are married. I wish it had been sooner. I'm sorry for that." She blew her nose and wadded the hanky between her palms. She laid her hand on her mother's arm. "Can you forgive me? I've wanted to ask so many times, and been unable. Please, Momma, please. I'll do anything you say, only please love me again."

"Kathleen, you're a child no longer. You know what you did, and I'll tell you again, I knew nothing of Josh's feeling for me before he asked me to marry him, but that wasn't what it was all about, was it?" Anne couldn't stop talking. It was like the bottom of the bucket had given way and a river of words gushed out. "It was your pride, and how it would look to the people in town, that's what worried you, not what it was doing to me, or Josh or your brothers and sister, only how you were going to look." Anne swallowed, took a deep breath and continued. "A few years ago I'd have worried what I was saying would drive you away but I don't worry any more. I found I can live without you, and enjoy it." She gave Kathleen a quick smile. "I'm saying more then should be said, but it's been bottled up so long there's no way to keep it in."

"I don't blame you, Momma, everything you said is true. What I did was terrible, stupid, but it'll never happen again. I can't tell you how I've missed you, how I've envied Ian walking in and out of my old home. I would have crawled on my knees to the backdoor if I'd thought you'd talk to me, but I let it go too long. I couldn't go back." Kathleen wiped her eyes again. "Remember when you came to see me and I wouldn't answer the door? I wanted to, but something stopped me, held me back. I was sorry the minute you left, and still I couldn't bring myself to ask you to forgive me. Everything you said is true." Kathleen sighed as she wiped her eyes. "It was all because of my pride, stupid pride." She looked at her mother, Anne's eyes were filled with tears. "Can you forgive me?"

"Oh, Kathleen, you think you can kiss the sore spot and make it all better? The scab will always be there, it's the healing beneath that takes the time and you've caused a deep wound." Anne shook her head, " I'm not saying I'm without fault. I should have known how you'd react, but it never once entered my mind. I love Josh Reynolds now; he's a good man, a good father to the boys and your sister. He's regretted not telling you the truth before he did." Anne looked at her daughter, the sun glistening on her hair. Kathleen looked no older than when she'd gotten out of school, she thought to herself. "No matter, it would have ended the same."

"Momma, they want to see me." Kathleen looked down at the envelope she was holding. She was almost smiling. "I've been in a state since I got it." Clearing her throat she looked shyly at her mother, "Why do you think they want to see me?"

'Kathleen, it was bound to happen, you've been writing since you first picked up a pencil. Let me see the letter again." Kathleen handed her mother the envelope. She stood watching her mother's face, hoping for a smile, anything that would show her mother had forgiven her.

"You must keep the appointment. Could be the chance you've

always wanted." Anne patted Kathleen on the arm. "We'll find someone to mind the bakery while you're gone."

Kathleen heard pleasure in her mother's voice. "Could you go with me, do you think?"

"Not that day. The accountants will be here." Anne thought for a minute. "What a shame Roseanna is married and gone, I know she'd love to go."

"I've not heard from her since they moved to Waterbury." Kathleen picked up her purse and inserted the check and letter. "I hope it works out well for them."

"Come, we'll have a cup of tea." Anne filled the kettle with water. "A good place to start, don't you think?"

Chapter Twenty-three

Emma trudged down Main street. Despite the blue wool sweater across her bony shoulders, goose bumps covered the back of her arms and shivers ran down her spine. She'd forgotten her key again, left it at home in the kitchen drawer. She'd have to wait until the other ladies arrived, in a half an hour or so, before she could get into the Sunday school room. She and Hortense would do the decorating this year while the older ladies frosted the Halloween cupcakes and set up the tables.

Giant oaks and elms lining the street were skeletons of their summer selves. Brown leaves had been raked into piles and set afire. Many a roasted marshmallow had stuck to little fingers and was eagerly licked away. The air was filled with the delicious smells of burning leaves, sliced pumpkins and baked apples. Traces of winter skittered through the air as elusive as the headless horseman. Emma looked up at the open blue sky. The robins and the geese had vanished, leaving the clouds free to wander.

She checked her watch. It was much too early to go to church but she didn't want to be late, the ghosts and scarecrows had to be hung before the children arrived at four.

She'd tripped over every bump in the old wooden sidewalk running down Main Street since she was a child so she had no need to look down. Pumpkins with triangular eyes sat on bales of hay, scarecrows with infectious grins leaned against haystacks and witches riding sidesaddle on flying brooms filled the store windows.

Halloween was everywhere.

The white gothic Congregational Church and the little brown Church in Christ sat across from each other at the end of the street. Geographically close, but theologically miles apart. Emma attended the Congregational Church.

She crossed the hard pack road to the Taft block and stepped up onto the wooden sidewalk. Shading a section of window pane with her cupped hand, face close to the glass she peered into the New England Power Company office. It was hard to believe a woman was working in there. Emma clicked her tongue to the roof of her mouth, a sound of wholehearted disapproval. What was this world coming to, women working all day in the same room with men!

She could hear a man's voice on a radio. He was talking about the war in Europe. So far President Wilson had kept America out of the war, but would he be as successful in 1915? Emma's husband said "No, we'll be in the war before the year ends." She hoped he was wrong.

She turned from the window as a car growled to life somewhere behind her. It was Rebecca in her dusty black Ford. She was the only woman in town who drove a car. Just like her, Emma snorted to herself. She rushed into the dry goods store, brushing against George Emory as the two tried to squeeze through the doorway at the same time. "Mornin', George."

"Mornin', Emma." He held the door open with his muddy boot. Emma didn't mind the odor of milk, cows and manure. Farm life had a comfortable smell, one she'd grown to like. She turned and looked toward the road. Rebecca was gone.

"You looking for something in particular, Emma?" Jessica Arnold sat behind the saloon length counter her knitting needles working as fast as her mouth. Her feet kept time to the music on the radio. She put her knitting on a shelf under the counter and waited as Emma browsed. She twirled the button at the top of her dress with her long, elegant fingers.

"Just nosing, Jess, looking for material for the girls, what with the holidays coming and all."

"Got some real nice fabric coming in on Thursday."

Emma couldn't get Rebecca off her mind. She'd never forget when Papa and Rebecca married. There were no more fun things alone with her Papa after that. No sitting in Papa's lap in the evening while he read to her, no more being the 'woman of the house,' no more deciding what they'd do on Sunday afternoons. Her lips tightened in a taut white line. Imagine calling that woman Momma. She wasn't her mother and never would be!

Jessica had returned to her knitting when Emma turned to her. "Got to go Jess or I'll be late."

"Going to decorate the church?"

"Uh-huh, be back to look at the material in a couple of days."

Emma cut through the recently renovated Commons. Newly varnished wooden benches gleamed in the sun. There wasn't a chip out of the black wrought iron arms or legs . A water fountain sat at the end of the path. The bandstand was gone. Why would they take the bandstand down? Where will courting couples go to be alone? Where were the eaves for birds to build their nests under? Where could children play jacks or jump rope when it rained?

Emma admired the white globes on the new electric lamps. No wonder kids got into trouble. The town should leave the street lights on every night, not just when there was no moon. Emma knew the trouble a girl could get into in the dark. She sighed audibly.

She put her hand up to her marcelled light brown hair, waved in the back with short bangs across her forehead. She'd been told it made her look younger than her twenty-nine years.

"Hey, wait for me!" Emma knew that voice; it was Hortense Burton Bocchino. The two had played together since they were in diapers. Hortie poked her arm through Emma's. "Why are you wearing that heavy sweater?"

Emma grinned at her old friend. "Gets chilly late afternoon, when the sun goes down."

Hortie leaned closer and whispered, "I heard something this morning might interest you." She paused, enjoying the moment.

"Oh, what?" Hortie always knew the latest gossip; her husband was Uxbridge's only barber.

"Not what, who." Hortie waited, Emma said nothing. "About Rebecca, your stepmother." Hortie loved gossip, particularly spreading it.

"What's she done now?" Emma tried to show no interest, or Hortie would drag this out for the rest of the afternoon.

"Got a boyfriend." Hortie cleared her throat. It didn't have to be cleared, it was her way of letting Emma know this information was very important. It was impossible to miss the gloating expression in her voice.

Forgetting her resolve, Emma stopped and turned to her old friend. "Who'd be interested in her, she's over forty?"

Hortie fumbled with the sleeve of her dress, unable to meet Emma's eyes. "I don't know, I just heard it this morning." She gave Emma's arm a tug, "Come on or we'll be late."

"Who would be interested in her?" Emma asked again, her resolve forgotten.

Voices and laughter were coming from the kitchen as they entered the Sunday school room directly behind the nave of the church. It was cool after the direct sunlight.

Hortie waited as Emma took off her sweater. "I'd tell you if I knew."

Boxes containing Halloween decorations covered the Lilliputian tables. Emma and Hortie removed paper witches, scarecrows, pumpkins and yards of orange and black paper chains which they tacked to the waist high wainscoting . The room smelled of musty paper, old dried glue and little children.

Emma's brows knitted together. It had taken a few seconds to realize the enormity of what Rebecca had done, if it was true. She could ruin them all; Emma's mother-in-law, Mrs. McDuff would never forgive or forget the disgrace her son had caused by marrying into the Hawley family There wouldn't be a child allowed to play with her children. How could Rebecca have done this to her!

Poor Roseanna wouldn't be able to live in Uxbridge again or

return to the farm, not after this. Rebecca could lose everything, including her daughter…everything.

"What are you thinking?"

Emma tacked a scarecrow below one of the links in the paper chain. "Do you think she'd really do that, have an affair?"

"How should I know? She should have more sense, but …" Hortie looked through the decoration box until she found a large smiling pumpkin, "She won't be able to live in Uxbridge if it's true."

"Promise you'll tell me if you hear something else?"

"As soon as I hear."

Emma tacked a scarecrow above the door frame. She stood for a moment, a paper witch in one hand, a tack in the other and stared at the wall, deep in thought. Rebecca wouldn't be that foolish, she knew what would happen.

The sun had reached the three stained glass windows on the west side of the room making a mosaic quilt of blues, reds, greens and yellows across the childrens' tables. It was hard to decide if the colors made the ghosts and witches come to life or appear more deathlike; red became orange, yellow became green, blue had turned to violet.

It was impossible to imagine Rebecca involved with a man. She could never hold her head up again, not here in Uxbridge. No one would speak to her; she'd be shunned wherever she went. And Rebecca's pride couldn't stand that, not Miss Perfect Rebecca, but where there's smoke there's fire and sparks would land on the whole family, burning everyone of them. Emma continued tacking ghosts and pumpkins to the wall. The more she thought the more she convinced herself it couldn't be true. It just couldn't. There was nothing a woman protected more than her good name and Rebecca would never do anything to lose that. Would this woman never stop causing her misery!

Chapter Twenty-four

"Oh my, she sounds happy, a two story house not far from the center of town." Anne was happy for both Roseanna and Rebecca; she knew how much Rebecca loved her daughter. "What do you suppose she means by 'it might need a little work' and why do they want such a large place?" Anne was talking to herself and didn't expect an answer. "Now, this makes more sense, renting out the second story." Anne peered over the top of her eyeglasses. "For heavens sakes, Becky aren't you going to offer me a cup of tea?"

Rebecca's expression was one of surprise, as if Anne were speaking a foreign language. "I was that anxious for you to read the letter I completely forgot. It came not an hour ago." Rebecca filled the kettle with water and set it on the front burner.

Letter in hand, Anne said, "Did you know Waterbury's the Brass Capitol of the world?"

"I thought they just made dollar watches." Rebecca set fresh rolls on the table. "No wonder they have so much war work with all those factories."

Anne pushed her glasses up. "It's nice to see a young couple start out on their own, ready to conquer the world so to speak, yet I can't picture our little Roseanna running a home of her own. Just yesterday she was bouncing up and down in your lap on the way to the farm, so small she was hidden in her blankets." With a voice filled with emotion Anne said, "Robert and David were with us then. A lifetime ago it was."

"More like a dream," Rebecca replied, her voice a whisper. "Would we have the bakeries and the restaurant if our husbands were here do you think?"

Anne's throat was so tight, so she couldn't reply.

A pleased expression on her face, Rebecca waited a moment before she cleared her throat. "We did what we had to do and made a darn good job of it," she said, "they couldn't have done better."

Annie shivered, quickly shelving memories to the back of her mind.

"They'd never have allowed it and it would've been too much for you with all you had to do at the farm and with my brood, I never could have done it." She reached for the sugar bowl. "But we managed when we had to and it's time now to get on with the future, no more dwelling in the past." An austere expression replaced the one of longing and she continued. "But there's one thing worries me, and I'm sure you know what it is, your having no husband. I know you have Richard, but he's far from a husband. " Anne blushed and lowered her head so Rebecca couldn't see.

"Not a husband, exactly but close enough," Rebecca replied. The teapot whistled and she turned off the gas. "Richard and I get along as we are. What more do we need?"

"Why don't you look for someone interested in marriage?" Anne pretended to be engrossed in the letter she was reading.

"I'm not sure I want anyone interested in marriage. My life is full enough as is. I have Roseanna and we have the bakeries and the restaurant. I hardly have time for more." Rebecca poured milk into her cup and stirred in a teaspoon of sugar. "I thought you liked Richard, why are you are trying to get rid of him?" This was said with no rancor.

"I think the world of Richard but I want more for you. You should be safely married, not have a man for convenience." Anne poured a small amount of milk in her cup and stirred. "Of course, you know Emma will be delighted if she gets wind of your affair and that's what it is. You may call it anything you wish, an engagement to marry, anything, but it's still nothing more than an affair. I grant you it's been going on for a time but I see no ring on your finger." Anne let out a terse giggle. "Can't you picture Emma rubbing her hands together and cackling over a boiling cauldron, witch that she is. Be careful of her, Becky, she can be dangerous."

Rebecca's palms circled the sides of the teapot. "Feels about right. Here, let me pour."

Anne had been feeling remorse about her remark about Emma. "I don't know why I say those awful things about Emma; she's always been pleasant to me, but I've seen how she acts with you and I've never liked it." Anne quietly sipped her tea, allowing herself time to think. "If this keeps up, the affair between you and Richard, one day you'll find yourself shunned by your neighbors and a daughter not speaking to you. 'Tis not a thing to be taken lightly."

"Richard and I take every precaution," Rebecca said. "There's no way anyone can know." Rebecca lowered her voice, as if someone might hear. She was unable to meet Anne's eyes. "There's no way you can judge our feelings for each other but obviously we must be happy with the way things are or we'd have changed them long ago."

Anne plunged ahead. "Has Richard asked you to marry him?"

"Many times, but I won't leave Uxbridge. Roseanna would be broken-hearted. You know how she loves the farm, and there's no way I can take care of business here and be in Boston at the same time." Rebecca picked up a roll and broke it in two. "As much as I'd like to there's no way it can be done."

"Ah, but Becky, Roseanna is happy and she's not on the farm or in Uxbridge. As for the businesses, don't you think I'm capable of managing alone a few days a week?" Anne sipped her tea with the angelic expression of a three-year-old.

"A wonderful lawyer you'd have made." Rebecca held the basket of rolls out to her sister-in-law. "And I suppose you're right; if Richard and I felt so inclined we'd have worked things out long ago." Anne set her roll on her bread plate.

Doing what she does so well, Anne changed the subject. "When are we going to Waterbury, you've not said a word and you know

I'm dying to see the new house."

"Emma and the girls have been visiting so it'll have to be after the holidays. I'm afraid to drive on these icy roads; we'll go by train and stay overnight."

Anne giggled like an excited teenager. "I'm dying to see the new house, aren't you?"

"You're not fooling me for a minute, Anne Reynolds...you'd do anything to get out of a day's work!"

The minute Roseanna and Grant saw the house they knew it had to be theirs.

Flagstone steps led from the mail box at the edge of the dirt road to the front door. The house, like the sprawling oaks surrounding it, appeared to have been there forever.

Clutching the back porch rail were the scrawny limbs of a magnificent lilac bush. Every year the bush was touched by the magic of spring and elegant green leaves burst into life as it exploded into clusters of lavender flowers; nature's daytime fireworks. Their odor was deeper than their color, permeating the yard and creeping unseen into the house. This happened sometime in May.

A wide porch hugged the first floor like a sleepy child cuddling a teddy bear. Two flagstone chimneys stood on either side of the house. Paint was chipped and shutters sagged but inside there were no telltale watermarks on the ceilings or walls. The basement was dry and the attic snug.

Grant and Roseanna had saved enough to pay half of the one thousand dollar asking price. It had been cheaper last year, but a year ago factories were manufacturing watches and brass products, not implements of war. Waterbury had a population of 52,000 people when the war began; it had since doubled, so real estate was becoming more and more valuable.

There was work to be done inside and out, but how could they lose? It would be worth triple what they paid by the time the war was over and they moved back to Uxbridge.

Chapter Twenty-five

Emma would never again think of the fifteenth of December as an ordinary day. It started out ordinary enough though the sky was melancholy and the air heavy and oppressive. It was Saturday.

The ice had been shoveled clear of snow by the time Emma and her two daughters, ten-year-old Georgiana and nine-year-old Velma arrive at Taft Pond. Four youngsters huddled over a small bonfire, red fingers thawing above the weary flames. Seven or eight teenagers played Snap-the-Whip in the middle of the pond. Youngsters trying their first pair of skates quickly found the unforgiving ice spares no head or rear.

Ice fishermen wearing warm trousers and heavy jackets squatted over holes they'd cut in the ice. They sat in silence on the far side of the pond waiting for their small red flags to 'tip up' and let them know a fish was on the line. These men were not wearing skates but had on thick soled rubber boots.

Youngsters slid down the log, making room for Emma and her girls. The day looked no more ominous than any December day except for the unbroken overcast. The children and fishermen seemed to feel the impending grief without being aware of what it was. The children were not as noisy, and the fisherman sat staring at the holes they'd drilled in the ice in a hypnotic trance. They were not yelling back and forth as they always did.

"How's the ice?" Emma asked.

"Little rough in the middle. Watch out on the far side, piece of wood, a limb or something is frozen in the ice." Emma blew on her fingers to warm them.

"Got any cookies, Mrs. McDuff?" Emma reached into her tote bag and hunted among dry socks and mittens before finding the bag of oatmeal cookies. She handed it to the children. The cookies were still warm.

Emma closed her eyes. Cold air with a hint of sweet smelling smoke from the smoldering logs filled her lungs. Despite the warm fire and happy laughter she was on edge, couldn't seem to relax as she waited for some unwelcome happening.

"Be right there," Georgiana yelled to her friend Kathryn and was gone before Emma had her skates laced or her mittens on.

Suddenly the laughter stopped. A shiver shot up Emma's back. All was still, the birds sat in the branches as if put there by a taxidermist. The ice was silent, no longer mumbling or complaining like an old man trying to get out of his chair. Icy air burned its way down Emma's throat. It was so still; no one looked at her but she knew everyone heard her frenzied breathing. Weightless snowflakes scampered through the air like children let out of school, as if nothing was wrong.

One of the boys yelled for a board. "Quick. Over here!"

Emma raced toward the group. Two fisherman, slipping and sliding in their boots, made their way toward the screaming children.

"Where's Georgiana?" Emma's voice was not far from a scream. Instinct told her it had happened to Georgiana. Velma sat on the log lacing her skates. No one answered Emma, they were busy looking at something in or under the ice. The men had made a human ladder, laying flat on their stomachs, inching the board as close as they dared toward the freezing black water.

A red jacket floated to the surface. Emma tried to get closer, but it was crowded and no one gave her room. She had trouble looking over their heads but was able to see Georgiana pulled from the icy water.

One of the fisherman hit her on the back as if she were a newborn and water gushed from her mouth. She was quickly wrapped in blankets. Her hands and feet were massaged. Color crept back into her face, her blue lips began to turn pink.

Next, ten-year-old Kathryn was pulled from the same black hole. She was thumped on the back but no water gushed from her mouth. Then she was stretched out on the ice, on her back. One of the men hunted for her carotid artery but there was no pulse to be found in her neck. There wasn't a flicker of an eyelash, no raspy gasp for breath. Kathryn looked like she was carved of wax. She was dead.

Years later, in her mind's eye, Emma could still see the men and boys stretched out on their stomachs, reaching into the freezing water, wrinkled blue hands grasping tree limbs, broken boards, anything they could find to snag a jacket, a hand or a leg. The icy water sopped their clothes and ran down their arms, under their clothing onto their warm skin. Grunting was the only human noise heard as the swirling water slapped against the jagged ice. The air was white with their urgent breathing. No one spoke.

A blanket covered Georgiana's chin. Emma pulled it up, almost covering her nose. Her breathing and color were returning to normal, but her eyes had the vacant stare of someone lost and unable to adjust to where they were or what had happened. She looked at her mother and tried to speak, managing only a weak smile. Emma touched Georgiana's face with trembling fingers. Now Emma knew how the mother lion felt in times of danger. She would have liked to pick up her cub and carry her back to the den, but how could she when her legs were so weak she couldn't stand?

How could she console someone who's only child was dead? What could she say to ease the pain? The Coopers were old friends, and their house would be so empty, there would be no Kathryn sounds heard again. Emma's head echoed with screams and sounds she never wanted to hear again. She shuddered every time she thought it could be her daughter who died and not her friend.

Emma had soaked in a hot tub of water and been rubbed dry by George who bundled her into a warm nightgown and wool slippers. He set a hot cup of tea in front of her. "Don't you worry, honey,

Georgiana will be alright."

Emma patted the chair next to her. "Sit next to me." She reached for a napkin in the holder. "It was awful. After that first terrible scream everything got so quiet. The only thing I heard were blades scratching across the ice as everybody raced to the other end of the pond." Emma looked up from her tea and smiled at her husband. "Death must enjoy my company, my father, my mother... can you feel my hand shaking?"

"Not true." George reached for her hand. "And you're not the only one shaking, feel my hand."

"I'm not sure if it's you or me." Emma's shoulder dropped as she began to relax.

"I keep thinking about the Coopers...oh, those poor people. What can we do?"

"Let them know we're here. There's little else."

Emma gave George a questioning look. "Isn't it odd I feel this deeply about friends, but if it happened to Rebecca..."

"Rebecca's been good to you, in her way." George filled the teapot with water. "There's blame on both sides, as I see it."

"Rebecca didn't hate me in the beginning, but she's never liked me very much either." Emma removed the handkerchief from her sleeve and blew her nose. "How did Rebecca get into this conversation anyway? Haven't I've enough on my mind without her!"

Chapter Twenty-six

Rebecca scooted down in the tub and closed her eyes, only her head could be seen above the bubbles. A helmet of tight red curls framed her face, thanks to the humidity. The Copley Hotel bathroom was filled with the scent of roses and steam. It was so quiet she could easily have fallen asleep. Water as soft as butterfly wings swirled about her legs. She continued adding hot water until the tub was about to overflow. The back of the tub was a sheet of ice on her back as she leaned against it.

The train had arrived early in Boston so she had an extra half-hour to soak before meeting Richard in the lobby at five-thirty. They often ate in the hotel dining room, but never spent the night here. They went to Richard's house. The highboy in Richard's bedroom held her nightgowns, underwear, hose, toiletries, even material for the quilt which she worked on in the evenings. The quilt was growing; soon it would be large enough to cover a full-sized bed.

She and Richard were careful not to be seen together, except for dinner in the hotel or in consultation at his office. They didn't have to worry at Richard's house. The garage was not far from the back door. It took Rebecca a few second to get in the house.

This was not some sneaky little affair. Neither was cheating on a spouse, they were both free to do as they wished. She loved Richard and he loved her. It wasn't that Richard hadn't asked her to marry him, he had; but how could she leave the businesses she and Anne had worked so hard to build? How could she leave the farm? Where would they spend their holidays, Roseanna and Grant, Anne and her children, Mary and Jim? It wouldn't be Christmas any place else. The farm was home to Roseanna, to them all. Rebecca's love for Richard had wrapped her in a gossamer trap.

She couldn't expect Richard to give up his law practice in Boston, he'd left Uxbridge for bigger things and there was no way she could give up Richard. They loved each other so much, didn't that count for something? One day they'd marry, they really would, when the time was right.

Anne kept saying, 'there's many a slip twixt the cup and the lip,' but she was wrong this time. There'd be no slip between she and Richard.

They laughed and enjoy sex; it wasn't hidden in the dark as if it never happened or happened to someone else. So different from David where sex was hidden, never mentioned. Was it because that was the way their marriage began and he was afraid to embarrass her? They'd never had time to really discover each other, to ask and listen.

Anyone not knowing them would assume she and Richard were married. They'd established routines the same as other married couples. Rebecca was first out of bed in the morning. She dressed and put on her makeup while he showered. By the time the towel was around his waist she was sitting on the corner of the bed where he could see her in the bathroom mirror, in the spot he kept rubbing clear of steam. He lathered and shaved as they talked.

Rebecca grinned. "There's a well known lady who also tried to rub out a spot, for a different reason, of course."

"Altogether different. I'm just keeping the lines of communication open." He tried not to smile. He didn't want to cut himself and have to cover his face with little white paper flags. He shook the doubled edged razor in the hot water and with his head tilted to one side put his fingers to his neck, just below the chin line and held the skin taut as the razor slid through the snowy shave cream. She'd seen him do it a hundred times; it was as much a part of their life as eating breakfast together.

Rebecca opened her eyes and reached for the hand towel. She wiped perspiration from her face and pushed her hair back.

It was impossible to imagine living in his large, old house where nothing had changed since Sarah, his first wife, died twenty years ago. Nothing had changed in that house for the past two hundred years for all she knew. In her minds eye she could see Sarah's kitchen, the black iron stove against one wall, the porcelain sink with legs as long and graceful as a ballerina, beneath the kitchen window. Sarah's everyday china and tumblers stacked behind the glass door cabinets, just as she'd left them. The most used drawers were lined with butcher paper. The seldom used drawers, the ones filled with string, thumb tacks, recipes cut from magazines and rubber bands, were lined with newspaper. Rebecca wondered if it was because newspaper was cheaper and Sarah watched her pennies, or she'd run out of paper and put in whatever was available. Sarah was a very neat housekeeper, much neater than herself. A gray braided rug, once yellow and green, stood in front of the sink. The linoleum was new. Richard had replaced it when the wood flooring began to show through. His housekeeper picked the colors and the pattern.

Sarah picked out the rugs, the drapes, the dining room set, everything. It was hard to believe she'd been dead so long. There were times when Rebecca thought the sheets still held the scent of Sarah. She wondered if Richard ever thought of Sarah when they made love. Probably not. Richard said it was all in her mind and he was right. Sarah had to be buried once and for all, Rebecca was the only one keeping her alive. If they ever lived in this big old house the first thing she'd do was an exorcism of Sarah. Out with the drapes, the rugs, the furniture. Everything. Richard had told her to change anything she'd like now. She'd like to do it, but felt Sarah might walk in and catch her and what would she do then? Richard wasn't keeping a shrine, he'd been too busy raising his son and practicing law to bother with the house.

She turned the faucet to 'H' and gave a sigh of relief as hot water hugged her feet, and slithered between her toes and around her legs.

She slid down and closed her eyes as she thought. Roseanna and Grant. It hadn't been easy since they moved to Waterbury. She missed Roseanna. And she couldn't help but wonder about the fire at Josh's lumber yard. The body they found showed he was from Grant's hometown: Bumbly, Virginia. Could he be connected to Grant in any way?

The fire started in one of the storage sheds. They were lucky it hadn't spread any further. It wasn't until the next day, after the ashes cooled, they found the body. Whoever it was must have fallen asleep with a lighted cigarette. With all the sawdust it was like putting a match to a parched bale of hay. The only thing they knew for sure was, he wasn't from Uxbridge. Not many strangers came to Uxbridge. There was nothing to come for unless to visit a friend or a relative and there'd never been a hotel. Could he have been passing through on his way to Boston or Canada?

Rebecca would be happy when Anne got back to the office. She'd been busy helping Josh and hadn't had a chance to catch up with the accounts, but it wasn't the accounts that bothered her. They could be caught up in no time. She missed seeing her, talking to her. They talked everyday, it was just…well, they hadn't had a cup of tea or a good gossip together in the past three weeks and she'd like to find out more about this man from Virginia.

Once the snow and ice melted Reynolds Park would be open and that took a lot of Josh's time. Chuck managed the park for Josh but all the decisions and a lot of the work were still done by Josh which left Anne at the lumber yard a day or two a week.

Ellen, Anne's youngest daughter ran the bakeries now that Kathleen was gone but Ellen was expecting her first child in three months. They'd manage somehow, they always had.

Rebecca inched down in the water. It seeped beneath her skin to the bones, warming her through. It was too comfortable, her arms relaxed and she closed her eyes.

Kathleen? At last she was doing what she always wanted,

writing, and was at peace with her mother. She'd been keeping company with an older gentleman — in his fifties she'd heard. Had Ralph left a scar that would never heal? Was that why she gravitated to older men? Or was she trying to replace her father or afraid of loving someone else? Only she knew.

Most every other weekend Ian came to Uxbridge to visit his grandma. He had a girlfriend now, and Kathleen was not happy; the girl was a Catholic. "A daughter-in-law with crucifixes hanging all over the house, to say nothing of Catholic grandchildren. No thank you!" Ian's wife would have to love him very much to have Kathleen as a mother-in-law.

Rebecca was afraid to add more water; the tub would overflow. Anne was right about her and Richard; they'd have to make some decisions soon, but not yet. It was too much to expect Anne to run the businesses almost alone and help Josh at the same time but there was no doubt Anne would be happier once she was married. She wanted her to be a respectable woman again, stop having to watch over her shoulder, afraid she'd see someone she knew. Anne was right. She didn't like it, but the alternative wasn't perfect either.

Rebecca wiped her hands on the towel and stretched her neck until she could see the clock on the nightstand in the bedroom. Fifteen minutes until Richard got here, better hurry.

She snuggled into a thick white terrycloth robe. The white octagon tiles were cool on her feet. Her hair had come loose and red ringlets cascaded down her back, making her look like a young girl. She dropped the robe on the edge of the tub and walked into the bedroom naked. An oil painting of the old North Church hung above the bed.

Rebecca's clothes and jewelry were on the bed. She dressed, her mind turning to Emma. Would she ever change, would the day come when she'd no longer be a volatile volcano, ready to erupt? She gets along well with others, why not me? I have done things with her I wish I hadn't, but nothing that would warrant this hatred. Maybe someday we'll be able to stay in the same room without acting like we were waiting for the bell to ring to come rushing out of our corners.

Rebecca pulled the blue tailored dress over her head and stood in front of the mirror. She hooked the clasp on the pearls Richard had given her around her neck and stepped back for an all over view.

She remembered seeing Emma get on the Boston train, not only once, two or three times at least. Not that Emma spoke or acknowledged her in any way, but why was she coming to Boston so often? I've got to ask Anne, she might know.

Chapter Twenty-seven

Jan. 11, 1916
My dearest Roseanna,

I've just gotten back from Boston and have tried to call
you, with no success. Anne was waiting at the station for me
with some very upsetting news.

I'm sure you remember the fire at Josh's lumber yard and
finding a body in the ashes of the storage shed where the fire
started. It didn't take long to identify the body as a
male...(As we have no woman tramps going through
Uxbridge, I could have told them that). They were still able
to read some of the papers in his wallet and know he is from
Bumbly, Virginia and his name is Harry Murray. Does Grant
know him?

Anne says there was a stranger asking around town if
anyone knew Grant. It doesn't take much to put two and two
together.

Roseanna, I am scared to death. You know what a disaster
it would be if anyone finds out the truth.

Please let me know what you and Grant decide to do.
Love, Mom

Jan. 13, 1916
Dear Mom,

You think you're scared!

Harry Murray is Grant's brother-in-law, his legal wife's brother. He and Grant were not close friends, nor were they enemies, as far as he knows. Grant says Harry was a lot older than Harriet, more like a father than a brother.

He left this morning to go to Bumbly to see what's going on. He will see Harriet on the off chance she has changed her mind and is willing to give him a divorce but he says not to get our hopes up as she's as stubborn as she is religious.

He'll call me every night. He should be gone two days at the longest. I'll call and let you know what's happening.

Love, Roseanna

Chapter Twenty-eight

The icy January wind sent a chill through Grant. He hunched his shoulders and pulled up his coat collar. Setting down his overnight bag he searched his pockets for his wool gloves. He was the only passenger getting off the train in Bumbly.

He stood scrutinizing the main street of the town where he was born. The town was set in a wide valley and was either hot and dry or cold and damp, there was no in-between. The sky was as clear today as Grant remembered from his childhood. Cloudless and vast and close enough so he could reach up and touch it.

Nobody was rich in Bumbly, but nobody was starving either, not with all the small farms dotting the countryside. The farms produced fruit and vegetables with a few chickens and maybe a cow for family use.

At this time of year there was little in the way of greenery on Main Street. The vintage wood buildings devoured paint faster than a camel at a watering hole. Remove the drug store at the end of the block and the whole town, all five stores, would collapse like a row of dominoes.

Grant walked to the south side of the station and rubbed a hole in the thin film of ice covering the window pane and peered into the stationmaster's office. The same dented coffee pot with the broken handle sat on the old wood stove behind Mr. Porter who was sitting at his desk, green eye shade on his forehead, wide rubber bands holding up the long sleeves of his white shirt, his bony fingers grasping a gnawed pencil stub. His hair was white now. Grant used to help Mr. Porter load and unload boxes when he was a high school kid, made a dime a week.

He had to wait for a car to pass before crossing the street to the drug store. The dirt road was waves of frozen ruts. The sign over the drugstore read, "Ben Brody and Bud Geyback, Pharmacists."

Bud's back was to Grant when he opened the drugstore door. He turned when he heard the door click and his face broke into a broad smile, "I had a feeling you'd be coming to town." He reached across the counter and shook Grant's hand in both of his own. "Good to see you, BG. You should have let me know you were coming."

"Your face get longer? Where's all that curly brown hair gone?" Grant was grinning as he said this.

"Same old wise guy. Sit down." Bud poured a little coke in the bottom of a glass and filled the rest with soda water. He set it in front of Grant. "If you're here for your brother-in-law's funeral you better high tail it over to the church." Bud looked at his watch. "Three o'clock right on the head."

"Who's the wise guy now?" Grant took a sip of coke. "Didn't have time to let you know I was coming, it all happened so fast. What the hell was Harry doing in Uxbridge and why was he sleeping in the lumber yard?"

Bud pulled over a tall four-legged stool and sat. "Who the hell knows with Harry? I was hoping you met some nice girl you wanted to marry and came to tell me or maybe you got a sudden yen to see Harriet? Which reminds me, Harriet's taken to calling herself Murray again, like you two aren't married anymore. Don't know if it means anything or not." Bud shook his head. "She was a great gal until she got all that religion." Bud paused and looked at Grant, making sure he wasn't offended. "I'd ask you to stay with us but you'd have to sleep on the couch and you'd wake up covered with kids and a drooling, half-breed dog. You'll be happier at the Green."

"Don't worry about it, just tell me what happened to Harry. What was he doing in Uxbridge?"

"Don't know. Everybody's been wondering." Bud paused. "I

always said there was something weird about that guy. Any guy who doesn't get married, for that matter." Bud pulled the four-legged stool closer to the counter and continued in a whisper, "Kept telling everybody you weren't going to get away with what you did to his little sister." Bud shifted and the stool squeaked. "Don't know what he was doing up there, but you can be darn sure he wasn't up to any good. Guess we'll never know, his burning to death. Can't help but feel sorry for the poor bastard, sorry way to go.

"Hell of a way to go. Wouldn't wish it on a dog. How did he know I was in Uxbridge, you got any idea?" Grant hadn't written Bud since he moved to Waterbury and he'd never told him about Roseanna. Bud could get careless particularly after a few beers. "Maybe he saw one of your letters in my pocket or on the counter and put two and two together. How the hell do I know?" There was a hint of defensiveness in Bud's voice. "No way to tell with a weird guy like that." Bud picked up Grants empty glass and set it in the sink. "We eat dinner about six, come a little before."

"No idea what he was doing there?"

"Who the hell knows."

Grant picked up his overnight bag and started for the door. "Got a room at the Green. Surprised the motel's still here. See you about five-thirty. Tell Carol not to fuss." Grant grinned. "Maybe a little, but not too much."

"Won't do any good, she'll fuss anyway."

Grant mailed Harriet's check to a post office box every month, so he had no way of knowing where she lived until last night when Bud told him she'd rented LaVarnes' old house on Maple Avenue. Grant knew the area well, he spent many hours playing kick the can and hide and seek on Maple Avenue. He stood for a minute, looking down the street. It hadn't changed, Herb Lenzo's house was still white with black shutters, looked like he painted it yesterday. The bird feeder was still on Tompkin's front lawn along with the drooling orange cat in the living room window. LaVarnes' house was at the end of the street, on the right, past George Trout's old place, where Benny and Walter used to live.

When he closed his eyes he could hear their voices. " Over here, Benny...come out, come out wherever you are... no cheating, Buzzy, you can't hide in your house...come on, Betty, it's getting dark we gotta go home." I wonder where those kids are now?

Bud said there was a sign in Harriet's window, "Dress Making/ Millinery." He took a few steps, his breath leaving a ghostly wake behind him. The temperature was in the low thirties. Frozen patches of snow squeaked beneath his leather soled shoes. That must be the house up there, it had to be. Same faded brown shingles and there was the sign in the upstairs window.

He had no hope Harriet would give him a divorce but he had to admit he was curious to see how she's changed after eight years. She'd been a vivacious, fun-loving girl when they'd first met. Voted Queen of the Prom, she was head cheerleader all four years, played clarinet in the band and was a straight A student. Everything was great when they first got married...until she discovered religion.

Grant stepped up on the porch of the tiny house and pushed the doorbell. Maybe she'd gained weight and was so big she'd fill the doorway. Would her dark hair be long or short, would she be as pretty as she had been? Eight years could make a lot of changes.

The high pitched ring echoed through the house, bouncing off bare floors and unadorned walls. He rang three times but no one came to the door. Maybe she wasn't home. He stepped to the parlor window and peered inside. Through sagging, white lace curtains he saw boxes, packed and ready to go. Vases of wilting flowers sat on the floor and squatted on top of boxes. Must be from Harry's funeral.

He was about to ring the bell again when he heard the tattoo of footfalls pounding toward the door. Harriet still walked as hard as ever on her heels.

Grant knew she wouldn't be glad to see him. She'd made it clear the last time they met that she never wanted to see him again. The feeling had been mutual, except Grant had held on to a thread of hope that Harriet would forget this religious stuff and come back to her old self or give him a divorce, but it hadn't happened. That was before he met Roseanna.

Bud had kept him up to date on what Harriet was doing and who she was doing it with. She hadn't dated since he left. Her brother Harry still lived in his apartment up on Rose Hill but spent most of his time at her house. From what Bud said, Harriet was fine, in church every time the door opened, taking in sewing and working at the general store four days a week and collected his checks once a month.

There was a small clicking sound. Grant looked down and saw the doorknob turn. He was still curious but another part of him wanted to run down the street, back to Waterbury and Roseanna, and never see Harriet again. He'd never loved her as he did Roseanna. Was it possible, as Roseanna said, she'd meet someone at church and would give him a divorce, or was it wishful thinking on her part?

The door opened and Harriet stood there looking at him. She wasn't smiling nor did she speak. If she'd gained weight it was nowhere to be seen. Her dark hair was cut a little shorter. Something about her eyes and mouth was different... tighter, more determined, maybe. She could walk under his arm if he raised it, so she hadn't gotten any taller. She was wearing a blue blouse, the same color as her eyes

Grant called in the opening. "You going to ask me in or not? I don't want to have to break the door down, but we're going to talk whether you like it or not."

"What are you doing here? I can't talk to you now, I'm busy packing." Harriet held the door open just wide enough for him to see her face, but her hand never left the knob. "Oh, I know, you came to express your condolences; well, save your breath." She hadn't forgotten how to be sarcastic. With that, Harriet tried to slam the door shut, but Grant grabbed the knob and refused to let go.

"Sorry to hear about Harry."

"We've got nothing to talk about. Go on back to Uxbridge or

wherever you came from and leave me alone."

Grant gave the door a hard pull and Harriet stepped back. Boxes were scattered up and down the hall.

"We've got unsettled business to tend to."

Harriet leaned against the wall. "You're wasting your time. What's the matter, you found somebody you want to marry?" Harriet didn't try to keep the mocking tone from her voice.

"We'll sit in here." Grant took her by the elbow and led her into the flower filled parlor. The old flowers were dead and musty smelling

"This is my house, BG, and I don't take orders from you!"

Grant started to sit on the loveseat than changed his mind and sat in the ladder back chair. "Nobody's giving you orders."

"You're not getting a divorce if that's what you want." Harriet pulled a handkerchief out of her skirt pocket. "You wouldn't dare come here if Harry was alive. If you think you can force me to give you a divorce you're wrong, I'm not afraid of you." She folded her arms and pretended to relax in the cushions.

She hadn't gotten around to packing the crucifixes yet, Grant thought to himself. His mother was right, crucifixes hung by the door, over the fireplace, even one sitting on the end table. Probably had candles burning in the other room too. "Harriet, let's try and do this peacefully. Yes, I want a divorce." He was surprised Harriet didn't try to interrupt him, "And you should too. You're young and attractive. You want a normal life, you want children. Why don't you give us both a chance?"

"You're afraid I'll ask for more money, that's the reason you're here. Nobody can live on what you send every month anyway." Harriet pulled her skirt down and crossed her legs with a decided snap. "Harry gave me money to help make ends meet." Tears filled her eyes. "I don't know what I'll do with him gone."

Harriet could always cry at the drop of a hat so he ignored her tears and said, "Looks like you're planning on moving. Where do you want me to send the checks?"

Harriet tied a knot in her handkerchief. "Same place, I'm not going far." She untied the knot and slipped the handkerchief back in her pocket. She pushed her hair off her forehead. "Father Boyd got me the job as housekeeper in the rectory. I'll have my own apartment, just one big room and a bath, nothing like this, but it comes with the job and I get all my meals. Of course, I have to cook dinner for him but I can still do my sewing. Can't put a sign in the window but it's mostly word of mouth anyway." She came as close to a smile as he'd seen.

"What happened, O'Brien get promoted?"

Harriet's smile disappeared. "For your information, Father O'Brien wanted to go back to Ireland and Father Boyd took his place and..." Harriet swallowed and took a deep breath, "everybody loves Father Boyd."

Grant leaned forward, the chair had begun to cut into his back. "How nice for Father Boyd."

"It's time you left, BG; I don't have to sit and listen to your sarcasm. You haven't changed one bit. I've heard it all before and don't need to hear it again." Harriet started to get up.

"You're right, I didn't come here to rehash old times."

"What's her name, BG? You must want to get married awfully bad to come all the way down here and beg. Is she pregnant, is that what it's about?" Lines of bitterness were beginning to form around her mouth and eyes. Maybe she's not as happy as she used to be with her precious religion.

"I don't have anyone pregnant, I just want to get on with my life, meet somebody and settle down. You should too." Grant leaned back in the chair. "You know the money won't stop if we're divorced, not unless you get married again and then you shouldn't need it. There's no reason you can't lead a normal life."

"Won't work, BG; I can have the money if I don't divorce you so why should I get married and give it up? Anyway, divorce is against my religion." She couldn't keep the offending smile off her face. "Remember saying 'till death do us part'? You'll get a divorce alright, over my dead body."

"Don't tempt me." He reached over and handed her Richard

Drummond's business card. " He'll know where to find me if you change your mind."

She turned from the door as she was leaving. "I doubt I'll need it," and dropped it in one of the open boxes.

Grant listened to her footfalls disappear up the stairs before he let himself out. He'd catch the one p.m. train to Penn station and then home to Waterbury, but first he had to say goodbye to Bud and Mr. Porter. That wouldn't take long.

He hadn't been surprised at what happened, a little disappointed but he hadn't expected anything else. Harriet would never change, but what could he tell Roseanna? He knew she wouldn't say anything for a few minutes, just look at him with those big, sad, tear-filled eyes. The hurt would leave him bleeding inside and trembling with rage. She had been sure Harriet would have found someone by this time; eight years was a long time. How was it possible Harriet could tell him how his life would be lived, why did she have the right to refuse him his freedom? What had he done that he and Roseanna couldn't live like normal people?

The only good news he could bring back was about Harry. If he'd been aware of Grant's marriage to Roseanna, all of Bumbly would have known, but they didn't and Harry would have made sure everyone in Uxbridge knew too, but that hadn't happened either, so Harry couldn't have known about Roseanna or he died before he could tell. Obviously he'd never discovered Grant and Roseanna were living together as man and wife, otherwise he'd have come to Waterbury, not Uxbridge. Maybe he'd heard something or was suspicious but died before he had the chance to say anything. With Harry dead, their secret was safe. According to Bud, Harry hadn't changed, he was still the same old loner who didn't confide in anyone. Good news, of course.

What exactly did he, Grant, have to offer Roseanna? Living a life of fear, afraid someone would discover they weren't really married? Bigamy? Would they put him in jail for that? You bet they would. How long would Roseanna be able to live with this uncertainty? Would she be able to do without children? It wasn't easy on Rebecca either.

Harriet hated him enough to never give him a divorce, and she'd never give up that check every month so even if she found somebody she probably wouldn't remarry. She'd already told him that.

If he and Roseanna had children they'd all be bastards. Innocent children suffering for what he'd done. How many people would this entangle before Harriet was through? He should give Roseanna a chance for happiness with someone who could give her a family, but how could he give her up? He loved her more than life itself.

Chapter Twenty nine

What a day to go to Boston, or any place for that matter. It was impossible to stand still when her feet were so cold, and her nose was running and she couldn't even find her handkerchief. She wished she were home. If it hadn't been so important she could have been in her nice warm house instead of out here, freezing. Rebecca made her life miserable even when she didn't try, Emma complained to herself. She peeked from behind the overloaded luggage cart, afraid her stepmother would see her. She was trying to be quiet and still. She was beginning to hate these trips to Boston.

Someone should have pulled the cart closer to the railroad station, out of the wind. Emma blew her nose, watching Rebecca to make sure she didn't turn and see her. So far the trips to Boston had been fruitless. Rebecca did nothing of interest. Emma was beginning to wonder if all the gossip was just that, gossip.

Rebecca stood in front of the station, near the tracks, bundled up in a black, wool coat belted about her waist. Wisps of red hair had escaped from beneath the blue cashmere scarf that covered her head. She shifted her small overnight bag from one gloved hand to the other, not because it was heavy but because the urge to keep warm demanded motion.

Emma waited until Rebecca boarded the train; she didn't want to sit with her, and certainly didn't want Rebecca to think she was being followed.

It had turned into a meringue world of snowflakes baked atop a winter pie. It was not the day anyone would pick to go to Boston, but Emma had no choice, she had to go, there was no other way to find if all the talk was true. The other two trips had done nothing to confirm the rumors that Rebecca had a lover. The only man Rebecca had been with was her lawyer and there was nothing unusual about that, that was the reason she went to Boston, to see her lawyer.

Emma recalled the first time she checked into the hotel. "Welcome to the Copley," the desk clerk smiled as he pushed the registry book across the counter for her to sign. He pointed to the pen. "Is this your first trip to Boston, Mrs. McDuff?"

"I'm meeting a cousin I haven't seen in many years," she told the clerk, "Would you check and see if Rebecca Hawley has registered yet?"

He flipped the pages of the tome she'd just signed, then rifled through the keys in the box above his head. "Your room is across the hall from Mrs. Hawley," he said as he handed her the key, "she hasn't checked in yet."

She was cautious, afraid of meeting Rebecca in the lobby, coming out of her room or at the elevator, but that hadn't happened. They met, by accident, in the dining room the first night she was there and Rebecca was with Richard Drummond.

Emma saw them before they saw her, but not in time to leave. Rebecca was looking at her, a surprised expression on her face. She turned and whispered something to Richard before nodding for Emma to join them. They gathered up the papers they'd been discussing to make room for her, but it was obvious they were having a business discussion so Emma thanked them and said "No, thank you anyway, I'm sure you're busy."

She ate alone, playing with her food and even ordered dessert, which was something she seldom did and had a second cup of coffee and Rebecca and Richard were still there with papers spread across the table, in deep discussion.

Emma had to see where Rebecca went after Richard left, so she waited in the lobby, sitting behind one of the pillars, until Richard said goodnight at the elevator. That was the last she heard or saw of either of them.

Rebecca didn't come out of her room that night. Emma kept her bathroom door shut when she ran water in the tub so she would hear if Rebecca's door opened or closed, but she heard or saw nothing.

Rebecca was either gone by the time Emma got up in the morning or she was still asleep, either way she was nowhere in sight, nor was she on the return train to Uxbridge the next day.

Emma had to admit she was disappointed, she'd hoped to see Rebecca with her lover but the only person she'd been with was her attorney, Richard Drummond. She'd been coming to Boston for more than ten years to consult with her lawyer. It was where she went and who she was with after seeing her lawyer that interested Emma.

Emma had the same room on her next trip. Everything was the same except Emma didn't eat in the Copley dining room. She saw no one go in or come out of Rebecca's room, not even Rebecca. Emma telephoned Rebecca's room after one o'clock in the morning and no one answered. Rebecca was a sound sleeper so she could have been there and not heard the phone ring. Emma hoped a man would answer but no one did so she hung up after a dozen rings.

What Emma really needed was someone to watch the door to Rebecca's room so she could get some sleep. But who could she trust to come to Boston with her? If they found Rebecca with her lover, would Emma's partner tell everybody in Uxbridge? Probably, and Emma didn't want anyone outside the family knowing. At least not yet. It could ruin Emma's marriage; George's mother would never let her forget who her stepmother was but that was a small price to pay compared to what else could happen. Anne and Rebecca could lose their businesses; no one would patronize them. Rebecca would be a woman with no morals, a whore they'd call her.

But Emma was not staying at the Copley this trip. She was staying with her friend, Jane Wallace. Jane had made Emma promise she'd stay the next time she came to Boston. She was anxious to show off the lovely old home she and her husband had bought and were busy furnishing. The house was not far from downtown and was on the bus line so it would be easy for Emma to get back to the Copley. Now that Emma knew Rebecca's schedule all she had to do was wait in the Copley until Rebecca left and follow her. She had to meet her lover some place, she wouldn't have the nerve to allow the man to stay in the hotel with her!

This trip started like all the others. Emma waited until Rebecca was on the train before she boarded. It wasn't crowded and Emma found an unoccupied seat next to the window, on the shady side. She slid across the green velvet cushion and set her overnight bag down, pushing it with her feet until it was under the seat in front of her. She'd barely settled when the train pulled out. White steam spit from the chimney as the train gained speed.

Suppose Emma did see them together and didn't recognize Rebecca's lover? Would it make a difference? If Rebecca was brazen enough to have an affair, was there anything she could say or do that would make her break it off? Should she tell Roseanna? Could Roseanna make her mother listen to reason or would it put a wedge between them, like Kathleen and Aunt Anne? Emma wanted to make Rebecca squirm, threaten her, anything to let her know how she felt. It would be sweet revenge for the past, for all Rebecca had done to her.

Suppose there was no lover and all this had been for nothing? It had to be true, why would anyone start such a rumor?

Emma had decided the family reunion on the Fourth of July would be the best time to confront Rebecca. Six months would be a long time to keep a secret of this magnitude, but well worth it just to see the look on Rebecca's face when she told her she knew about her lover. She'd like to be able to confide in Jane, but she couldn't, Jane knew so many people in Uxbridge and what would Jane think of her, having a stepmother like Rebecca?

The stark winter landscape rushed passed as if she was looking through a sterescope. Pine branches bowed under the weight of snow so white it hurt her eyes. It was a typical winter day in New

England.

Emma relaxed into the cushions and closed her eyes. She remembered the fear and excitement of that first trip, afraid of being caught, afraid what she'd find, afraid of finding nothing, but mostly fear of the unknown. But it hadn't stopped her.

Once off the train she stayed a safe distance behind, almost losing Rebecca when her bag got wedged under the seat, but she managed to catch a glimpse of Rebecca's red hair as she rushed into the station. The blue scarf was around Rebecca's neck, she hadn't pulled it on her head yet.

Rebecca hurried ahead and disappeared inside a two story granite building. Emma knew she was going to the second floor, to Richard Drummond's office. No point in waiting here, Rebecca would go from here to the Copley and dinner, but this time Emma would be waiting.

Emma took the streetcar to Jane's house. The snow was no longer as heavy but it had gotten colder. Wind from the ocean whipped through the Boston streets cutting her to the bone. Emma had told Jane she had shopping to do for the girls, so she'd be leaving after she got unpacked but would be back early in time for dinner. She felt sure Jane wouldn't come with her, particularly in weather like this.

Jane's house was warm, with fires crackling in the dining room and living room. The fireplace in Emma's room was laid with kindling, but had not been lighted. Emma's bedroom was on the second floor and had two large windows overlooking the tree lined street. The houses across the road were also two story structures with the same weatherbeaten elegance.

"What a lovely home you have!"

"Jack says it was built before the Cabots and the Lodges moved to Boston," Jane laughed, "but I doubt it." She opened a drawer in the highboy. "Put in whatever you like and there are empty hangers in the closet." Whenever Jane smiled, her brown eyes softened. "I decided to wait before lighting the fire, unless you want it now."

"Let's wait. Show me the rest of the house." Emma set her bag on the window seat. "Who lives in the house across the street?"

"The house directly across is a family by the name of Woodward, been here for years, the one on the left, the white one with green shutters belongs to an old Uxbridge native. You remember Richard Drummond, the lawyer, moved to Boston a number of years ago." Jane leaned over and peered down at the house. "Sad, we heard his wife died a few years after they moved in. His son's in college somewhere in New Hampshire, so he lives alone in that big house."

"Of course, I know him, he's Rebecca's lawyer."

"I'll give you a chance to wash up before I show you around. The bathroom's at the end of the hall and your towel and facecloth are already there. You've got the bathroom all to yourself." Jane blushed. "We have our own bathroom, right off the bedroom."

"I'd like to wash up first." Emma took out her toothbrush and paste. "I can find my way down the hall, you don't have to wait."

"Come down as soon as you're ready, I'll be in the kitchen." Jane put her hand on Emma's shoulder. "Do you really have to go out in this weather?"

"I'll be fine, it's not far to the streetcar and we have all day tomorrow to catch up."

As Emma stood looking out the window a two-door black car crept down the snow covered street, chains clinking as it inched its way along. It slowed before turning into the Drummond driveway. Drifting snow had hidden the road, but the driver didn't hesitate, he knew the way so well he could have found it blindfolded. The car crawled forward, coming to a halt in front of the garage at the end of the driveway. A man in a brown overcoat and hat got out. He reached for the shovel he had left propped against the side of the garage door and cleared away the snow before opening the heavy wooden garage doors and inching the car into the dark shelter. The door on the passenger's side opened and a woman got out. The man waited while she walked around the back of the car and joined him. Together they stepped into the falling snow. He cupped her elbow as if his hand was balancing a delicate piece of crystal and continued holding her arm, oh so gently but firmly, letting the world know this wonderful creature was his.

The woman stopped and said something to him. Little puffy clouds appeared and disappeared as they talked. The man turned and walked back to the garage while she waited. He returned carrying a small overnight bag. They laughed, making more white puffy clouds. He put his arm around her waist. They were hidden from the street by his house, but Emma could see them from her window. They made no attempt to move apart. The woman leaned into him. They stood for a moment gazing at each other in wonder. There were no small puffy clouds of conversation now. The man's hat had fallen to the ground, and lay in the snow. The woman reached up and pushed hair off his forehead, out of his eyes. He took her hand and held it, his eyes never leaving hers.

Emma sank into the cushioned window seat. A sigh escaped her lips. When was the last time she and George looked at each other like that? Emma's hands became tight fists in her lap; her breathing had almost stopped. She couldn't take her eyes from the scene across the street.

The snow had stopped, all sounds had become muted. The woman stood on tiptoe and put her arms around the man's neck. She buried her face in his neck. Emma closed her eyes, she could smell the masculine smell of him, feel the scratchiness of his beard. The man lifted the woman off her feet and held her against him. They were so absorbed in each other it would have made no difference if a shot had been fired, they wouldn't have heard.

They stood like a silhouette on a Valentine card. He touched her face, her hair, he tilted her chin so they were looking into each other's eyes. As gently as a butterfly hovering above a rose, his lips touched her lips and lingered. They were unaware anyone was watching, nor would they have cared. There was no room for others in their world.

The blue cashmere scarf she was wearing lay in the snow next to his hat, forgotten.

There was no doubt, it was Rebecca... but it couldn't be. And Richard.

Emma was speechless. The emotion of the scene had left her shaken. She'd been looking at Rebecca's lover all the time and never saw him.

Emma couldn't see the back door of the house, just the side. She watched lights go on and off in the kitchen, the front room and finally the upstairs bedroom.

Suddenly the house was in darkness.

Chapter Thirty

"What time are we coming home on Sunday?" Grant watched as Roseanna packed their suitcase.

"I want to get there Friday afternoon so I can help with the party. Saturday's party day and Sunday is talk about party day. Of course, we can leave early if you want." Roseanna put Grant's pajamas and her nightgown in the bottom of the suitcase but she never stopped talking. "The Fourth of July is a great day for a birthday, not that you need an excuse for a party, but everyone is out of school or on holiday." She picked out three pair of Grant's socks and put them in the suitcase. "What time will you be home tomorrow?"

"In time for lunch, then we leave." Grant grinned. "And what do you mean we can leave early? I'd have more luck pulling a wild cat out of that house. Between you, your mother, your Aunt Anne, Emma and Mary I don't stand a chance in hell." Grant found it impossible not to chuckle. "You're just lucky Josh and Richard are such good company." Grant stretched out on the bed, his head propped on his hand. "Who's going to be there?"

Roseanna removed their underwear from the bureau drawer and put it in the suitcase. "Nobody special, not like the year you came," she said with a mischievous wink. "Aunt Anne and Kathleen of course, because it's their birthdays, and the rest of Aunt Anne's family, everybody but Josh who's going to be at the park, but he'll be there later. It's a busy day for him. He should get there in time for dessert. Emma and George are coming with the girls. I hope

Emma and my mother can stay out of each other's hair. It's so touchy when they're together. I'm always waiting for one of them to explode. And that's the only people I know of. Of course, there could be somebody my mother hasn't mentioned."

Roseanna started to pack a small lavender can of dusting powder. She sniffed the top before turning the lid so the talcum couldn't escape and slipped it into one of the suitcase pockets. "My mother's so funny. She's finally finished the quilt, the one she's been working on since before I was born." Roseanna leaned against the highboy, a dreamy expression on her face. " I know where all the pieces are from; my baby clothes, my first school dress, my first dance, Papa's shirts, Mama's wedding dress and even some small pieces of material from the dress she wore the day she arrived in this country." Roseanna walked over and closed the lid on the suitcase and sat on the bed next to Grant. "I'm thinking of starting my own quilt so we can see our family history too, then when I have a blue day I can crawl under the quilt and touch all the happy times we've had." Roseanna reached for Grant's hand. "But first I have to have a daughter. What good is it if I'm the only one who knows the story behind every scrap of material?"

Grant pulled her down on the bed. "One day you'll have your daughter, if I have to strangle Harriet… and what a pleasure that would be."

"I almost forgot to tell you, mother said your friend Bud called. You're suppose to call him back after nine this evening. At the drug store." Roseanna got up from the bed. "I wrote the number down, it's next to the phone."

"I'll give him a call later; probably somebody died or ran off with somebody's wife." But Grant's expression was puzzled. Talking more to himself than Roseanna, he added, "The drugstore will be closed at nine. What the hell could have happened in Bumbly he doesn't want anyone to overhear?"

Grant sat on the sofa and stared at the paper with the phone number scrawled across it in Roseanna's "who the hell cares" handwriting. It was eight-fifty, a little too early to call, he'd wait a few minutes. What could have happened? In the past Bud had sent penny post cards when somebody died or ran off, which was pretty big excitement in a town as small as Bumbly. Grant looked at his watch. He'd wait an extra five minutes. If anyone was there, hanging around the drug store, this would give Bud time to get rid of them. At exactly nine-oh-five he picked up the phone and gave the number to the operator.

Was it possible someone in Bumbly discovered he and Roseanna were living as man and wife? Oh, God, he hoped not! That damned Harriet, how long could she go on making their lives hell, when would it end?

Like a ball of molten metal, fear and anxiety burned its way down to the pit of his stomach.

At seven minutes after nine the phone rang. Bud answered on the first ring.

"Bud, this is Grant. Heard you called." Grant stretched out on the couch, feet up, head propped on a pillow. Maybe Bud's gossip was nothing more than a joke he'd heard and couldn't keep to himself, or local trivia he thought might be of interest, but deep down Grant knew it was more serious than that or Bud would have sent one of his famous postcards.

"You better get yourself to a lawyer." Bud was talking so fast his tongue had gotten tangled in his southern drawl.

"What the hell's wrong?"

Bud waited. Grant's anxiety pulsated through the phone lines. "You're not going to believe it," Bud said, "I sure as hell didn't, she's sent the whole town into shock."

"What the hell happened?" Grant sat up, both feet on the floor, knuckles white as he grasped the phone.

"Harriet's gone," Bud whispered. "Remember she moved into the rectory a while back?"

"She's free to go any place she wants. Yeah, she was packing when I went to talk to her. Said she was moving to the rectory at the Catholic church." Grant's palm was wet and stuck to the telephone. He rubbed it down the side of his pant leg as he held the phone in his other hand.

"She was doing a lot more than housekeeping."

"What the hell are you talking about?"

"They've disappeared, Harriet and Boyd. All her stuff's gone and so is his."

"They left together… with each other? Come on, she'd never do that, it's against her religion. She'd be a fallen woman, shunned, people will cross the street rather than talk to her. Boyd's a priest for God's sake, they're not suppose to have those kind of feelings." There was silence as Grant tried to make sense of it all, "When did they leave, how long have they been gone?"

"Day before yesterday. Hell, Harriet was in and bought some aspirin that same afternoon. Folks saw her down street as late as five o'clock. Lights were on in the rectory till after midnight, they tell me. Probably packing, and they're gone, lock, stock and barrel."

"Hard to believe Harriet, with a priest! No wonder the town's in shock."

"All I know is they're both missing." Bud laughed. "She got religion alright, more religion than we ever thought. Wonder if this was going on when you two were together?"

Grant's head was spinning. "You're not pulling my leg, are you?"

"Hell, no. I tried calling Harriet's mother but she's locked up in her house, not answering the phone. I doubt she knows anything anyway, and they aren't answering the phone in the rectory either. It's one hell of a mess. All the Catholics are lying low, act like they're deaf, dumb and blind if you mention Harriet's name."

"I'll call my lawyer first thing in the morning." Grant took a handkerchief from his back pocket and wiped his face. "I'll give you a call, let you know what happens, if you hear any more you call me. Here's my new number; I'm living in Connecticut now, not far from Uxbridge." Grant thought about telling Bud about Roseanna but decided to wait. "Don't know how the hell to thank you for calling."

"What's going on," Roseanna called from the kitchen. "I can hear you yelling all the way in here."

"Got something to tell you." Grant hung up the phone and sat for a minute, stunned.

Roseanna dropped the dishtowel and rushed to Grant. "You look like you've seen a ghost."

He took her by the shoulders and held her at arms' length. "The ghost of marriage past. You want to get married, I mean really married?"

"Don't say things like that unless you really mean it." Roseanna wasn't sure what was happening but she knew it had to be good or very bad. "What's happened? I don't know if you're happy or sad, or crazy or what."

"Harriet's run off, eloped, which means we can get married, I mean really married." Grant had the biggest grin she'd ever seen. "You'd never guess who she ran off with."

" If Harriet has run away I hope it's with an Eskimo or somebody from New Zealand or so far away she can't find her way home." She took him by the hand and led him into the kitchen. Roseanna set two teacups on the table. "Sit down and tell me everything, word for word."

Grant pulled Roseanna's chair closer to his. "Harriet ran away with the priest, the one she was keeping house for."

"You can't be serious. She didn't!"

"From what Bud says she did. I'll call Richard first thing in the morning, I'm pretty sure I know what I can do, but I want to hear it from the lawyer's lips before I go off half-cocked. I want to be sure." Grant got up and pulled Roseanna to her feet. He put both arms around her and gave her a big hug. "I want to go to sleep knowing we're really going to be married... soon."

"Grant, you're breaking me." Roseanna stepped back, a bewildered but happy look on her face. "Why does it make any difference; she can still say no she won't give you a divorce and we're right back where we started."

"As long as she refused to give me a divorce there was nothing I could do. If she didn't agree we'd have to go to court and I'd have to prove she committed adultery which isn't easy, even if she did, but now, running away with a guy, that's all the proof I need. She won't dare fight me."

"But suppose you can't find her, what do we do then?"

"All I do is put an ad in her local paper, saying I won't be responsible for her debts and I start divorce proceedings. She has a few weeks to answer. If she doesn't answer, that means she's not contesting the divorce and, believe me, she won't contest it now. That's the divorce through the state. To get a divorce through the Catholic church take years…unless you have lots of money. The Pope overlooks a lot when he see that green stuff, but that's her problem, she's the Catholic, not me. For me to make it legal, I have to go through the courts wherever I live, like Virginia or Massachusetts or Connecticut."

Grant held Roseanna's hand. "I know it sounds complicated but it's not. Unfortunately, I was the one who left her, and for good reasons; it was foolish on my part but I couldn't stand it anymore. When we were first married, life was pretty good. Then she began spending all her time in church or at her mother's. I was working, taking care of the house, doing the cooking, the laundry, everything. Once in a while she'd fix a meal. I have lots of other complaints, but none good enough for a divorce."

Roseanna poured hot tea into their cups. Grant continued to talk. "If she'd agreed to a divorce we could have found a reason, particularly as there were no children, probably gotten it annulled, but she refused even that. But now that she's run away with this guy, priest or not, any court will say that's adultery and adultery is a good enough reason any place in the world." Grant blew on his tea trying to cool it down.

Roseanna began to cry.

"I thought you'd be happy." Grant reached in his pocket, took out his handkerchief and wiped away her tears.

"I am happy. I want to call my mother, she'll be as excited as we are."

Grant continued to hold her hand, he did not smile. "Roseanna, I want to be the one to tell your mother. I know we can't announce it but I want to tell her Friday night when the three of us are alone, before the party. I want to see her face."

Chapter Thirty-one

Rebecca couldn't help but smile as she looked across the kitchen at Anne who was sitting at the counter, licking chocolate off her fingers as she tried to balance on a three legged stool. It was like watching a sailor pick his way across the oil slick deck of a boat in a rough sea. A chocolate covered knife rested on the edge of the counter. "Do you know how many birthday parties we've had here?" Rebecca asked.

Anne licked more chocolate from her fingers. "Sometimes it feels like a hundred and twenty." She dropped the knife in the empty bowl and carried it to the sink. "Goodness, does it seem possible Kathleen's thirty-eight years old today?"

Rebecca stepped back from the table and shook her head. "Every year I'm afraid we'll run out of food, even with everybody bringing something, to say nothing of all the ice cream the children have churned, and when it's over I always wonder what we'll do with the leftovers." Rebecca sprinkled more coconut on her cake. "But if it's like other years, there won't be many a crumb left." Rebecca walked over to Anne and leaned down. She lowered her voice dramatically. "I've got something to tell you, but you can't say a word."

Anne wasted no time drying her hands on the dishtowel. She turned to her sister-in-law, expectantly.

Rebecca whispered, "Grant's wife ran away with a priest so now they can get married, I mean Roseanna and Grant. Don't say anything, 'cause you're not supposed to know."

"Ran away with a priest!" Anne whispered, stunned by the news, "For heaven sakes, why would she run away with a priest? "

"I don't know and I don't care as long as Roseanna and Grant can get married." Rebecca ran her hand across the counter making sure it was dry before she leaned her hip against it.

"If his wife comes back, will Roseanna and Grant still be married?" Anne was cautious where the law was concerned. "Can she cause more trouble?"

"Won't make a smidgen of difference, she's committed adultery. Running away with a man, and a priest is a man, is an automatic admission of adultery, she's the guilty party, so there's nothing she can do to stop Grant from divorcing her. Isn't it wonderful?"

"'When one gets up the other sits down, that's what makes the world go round' my grandmother used to say that and it's certainly true." Anne nodded her head and smiled, "I'm delighted for Roseanna and Grant. The whole thing has been ridiculous, but what else can you expect when you marry one of those Catholics!"

Rebecca agreed and added, "I'm sure Grant thought he was doing right when he agreed to marry in her religion but it's over and done with now and he and Roseanna can get on with their lives. Just think, once they're married I can have grandchildren."

"And what a treasure they are." Anne walked to the counter, bent down and eyed her cake as a jeweler would a precious gem. "When will they be getting married?"

"As soon as the divorce is final. Of course, we can't invite people to the wedding or even tell them about it. They're getting married in New York City and spending the weekend but I want to be there; I'll never get a chance to be 'mother of the bride' again."

"I don't blame you, but I hope you have sense enough to leave and let them have the weekend to themselves." Anne pushed her cake further back on the counter and without hesitation added, "Have you thought of making it a double wedding?" Her head remained bent, unsure how Rebecca would take her last remark.

"You always have the most wonderful ideas, but why did you

wait so long to ask, if only you'd said something sooner…" Rebecca never cracked a smile, leaving it to hover about the corners of her mouth.

"And what's wrong with getting married, may I ask?" Anne straightened up and looked Rebecca in the eye.

The screen door banged as Grant came into the kitchen. "Need any help?" He stopped and looked at the two women. "Am I interrupting something?"

"Not a thing, we were getting ready to clean up when we got the giggles." Rebecca set more dirty dishes in the sink. "Is everything ready outside, all set up?"

"We need a few more chairs."

"Take those over there, the two against the wall." Rebecca indicated two straight-backed chairs by the door.

With Grant gone Anne whispered to Rebecca, "Talk fast if you've got more to tell me, I don't want to miss anything."

Rebecca hadn't intended telling Anne, but she was at the bursting point, after all, half the pleasure of good news was the sharing, how could she possibly keep this from Anne any longer? Anyway, everyone would know in a short time. Rebecca put an arm across her shoulders and whispered, "Richard and I are married."

Anne grabbed the counter with both hands. "Oh my, and my hearing must be going."

Rebecca tried not to smile and failed. "We were married two weeks ago."

Both hands sprang to her mouth as Anne's eyes widened. "And never a word to me! You know I couldn't be happier. You'll never know how I've worried someone might see you together." Her words faded before she began again. "You need a man, someone your own age, someone who will take care of you. We have each other, but it's a wonderful feeling to have a loving husband by your side." Anne didn't come up for breath. "And what did Roseanna say when you told her?"

"She doesn't know; Richard and I thought we'd announce it after dessert, while we're having coffee. I wanted to tell her but

Richard didn't want his son to feel left out, so we decided to wait and tell everyone at the same time." Rebecca gave Anne a shy smile. "You don't know how it's been killing me not being able to tell you."

"When and where were you married?

"Vermont, two weeks ago. We thought it best in case anyone had seen us together; they'd never think to look at records there and there's no way we can be sure if anyone saw us together or not. You know how people are." Rebecca suddenly stopped talking.

"Why are you frowning?"

"It just struck me when I said that, about somebody seeing us together. Funny how things stick in the back of your mind and suddenly you start putting two and two together. Time and again I've thought back and wondered. It seems every time I got on the train to Boston I'd see Emma; she'd be hiding behind the luggage cart or the corner of the depot, some place where she could see me but thought I couldn't see her. I didn't think much of it at the time as I'm sure she's no more anxious for my company than I am hers. We even met in the Copley dining room one evening, and we asked her to join us but she refused. Then she lingered and lingered over dinner. I couldn't imagine why, she was alone so why stay in the dining room, a lone woman, unless she was meeting someone who never showed up or she was waiting to see where we went. I know I sound overly suspicious but what other reason could she have? We had to be so careful, we were so afraid someone would see us, and with Emma, who can tell what she was up to. She was even acting weird for Emma."

"Odd, I agree. Did she leave before you, in the dining room I mean?"

"Yes, as a matter of fact she did. Richard and I decided not to take any chances. When we left the dining room, Emma was behind one of the pillars in the lobby. She appeared to be engrossed in the newspaper. I remember thinking it was stupid to sit in the lobby reading when she could be in her room, relaxed in a clean pair of pajamas, just like at home. Something even odder than that; when

I checked in, the clerk told me a relative I hadn't seen in a long time had asked about me. She was staying at the Copley, had a room on my floor in fact, but he couldn't remember her name and I never heard from her.

"Richard and I said goodnight at the elevator and he left, like he was going home. I rode up to my floor, got off and walked the three flights down to the lobby. Emma was gone, the lobby was almost empty. Richard was waiting for me across the street." Rebecca rubbed her hands together as if they were cold. "I'm not saying she was spying on us; what I'm saying is it was peculiar and now when I think about it, it seems I saw her every time I went to Boston. Whenever I turned around there was Emma."

"Probably nothing to it; she goes to Boston to shop and has friends there, maybe she just happened to pick the same days as you."

"That's possible. I was suspicious of everything and everybody," Rebecca said, happy that that part of her life was in the past. "We're going to say we were married by a justice of the peace, which we were, but we aren't going to say when or where. We'll be misleading if need be and I'm not above telling an outright lie if anyone asks."

"And if that doesn't work, we can always put a little arsenic in Emma's tea," Anne added as casually as if she was giving Rebecca a new recipe.

"I can see you're going to be a great help." Rebecca giggled.

Anne and Rebecca were seated across from one another at the kitchen table, their bib aprons still in place. "Speaking of Emma, what time are they supposed to get here?"

"I expected them before now." Rebecca leaned back in her chair.

Anne walked to the sink and washed more chocolate off her elbow. "Getting rid of chocolate is worse than getting rid of sand, but a lot tastier." She picked up a towel and dried her arm. "Speaking of Emma, I still get chills whenever I think how close she came to losing Georgianna."

"Emma handled that situation very well. I'd probably have gone to pieces." Rebecca examined the cake and turned to Anne. "Think we need more frosting?" She pointed to the right side of the cake. "There?"

Anne bent down to look. "A little more all over can't hurt."

The backdoor slammed shut. "We got everything set up, except for the paper plates and napkins, but the chairs and tables are ready." Roseanna looked at her mother. "What time are Emma and George suppose to get here?"

"Any minute, we can set the food on the table. I'm sure they'll be here by the time we're ready to sit down." Rebecca wondered about the questioning expression on Roseanna's face. "Emma's bringing bread and rolls and she said something about a salad. Why are you looking so puzzled?"

"No reason," Roseanna laughed, "it's just that Emma and George are usually the first ones here and Emma never brings salad, she makes terrible salad." Roseanna turned and started out the door. "Oh, I think I hear Georgiana's voice now," she called over her shoulder.

Chapter Thirty-two

The past week, Emma's stomach had given her trouble. Probably due to nerves, what with the Fourth of July birthday parties coming up on Saturday. She wasn't sure how to approach her stepmother but one thing was certain, she'd tell Rebecca she knew she had a lover, that she'd seen her going into Richard's house and not coming out until the next morning. She wanted to tell her she'd seen them embracing but she couldn't, just thinking about it made her cheeks burn.

Emma would never forget the two of them, the shimmering snow dancing around their heads as they kissed and clung to each other; it was engraved in her mind, a permanent photograph.

She thought back to the trips to Boston, staying up all night waiting for a man to go into or come out of Rebecca's hotel room and Rebecca not even there! How she struggled to stay out of sight at the railroad station, afraid Rebecca would see her and trying not to lose Rebecca once the train arrived in Boston. No matter where or how long she followed, Rebecca always returned to Richard's law office.

She shook her head in disgust. It was a good thing the truth hadn't been a bear or she'd have been eaten alive.

She could hardly wait to get home and tell George. It seemed so long ago, telling George, first making him promise not to say a word. He was stunned and kept asking if she was positive it was Rebecca and Richard she'd seen. "After all, it was snowing, they were across the street, the window might have steamed up and visibility couldn't have been good. How could you be so sure?"

"Well, if it wasn't Rebecca, the woman was wearing Rebecca's coat and dropped Rebecca's blue cashmere scarf in the snow. How can you explain that?"

Emma set the bag of baked goods on the kitchen counter before giving Anne and Rebecca a peck on the cheek. "The girls will be in in a minute, they're talking to Roseanna and Grant." Emma opened the packages and took out some bread and rolls. "Hope I brought enough."

"We've got enough to feed an army...like every Fourth of July. Smells wonderful, did you just take them out of the oven?" Rebecca turned from the sink and looked at Emma. Emma seemed tense, like a cat who'd been watching a mouse hole and knew it was time for the mouse to appear. What now? Rebecca thought to herself.

"Almost." Emma looked at the desserts lined up on the counter. "The cakes are gorgeous, it's almost a shame to eat them. What can I do to help?"

The atmosphere in the room was pleasant, but there was something in the air... as if they were waiting for a balloon to break. Rebecca wondered if Emma could feel it. Probably not.

"Everybody's here now, so we're ready to eat." Rebecca picked up a tray of condiments and started out the door. "Somebody bring the salt and pepper please."

Emma had to run to catch up with her, a basket of bread and rolls in one hand, salt and pepper shakers in the other. "Rebecca, I'd like to talk to you for a minute."

Rebecca set her tray on the table. Why did Emma always do things like this, couldn't she see how busy they were?

"Can it wait until later?"

"It won't take long." Emma set the breadbasket and shakers on the table. Taking Rebecca by the elbow she led her away. "Let's go down to the river where we'll be alone. It'll only take a minute."

Rebecca shook her arm free." Is something wrong, George and

the children alright?" Rebecca asked as they crossed the new cut grass.

"Fine. I wouldn't insist if it wasn't important. As I said, it'll only take a minute."

They sat facing each other on the wooden seats of the old swing overlooking the Mumford river. Rebecca waited for Emma to say something but Emma seemed to have lost her nerve. Rebecca clasped her hands together and dropped them in her lap. "What do you want, Emma? I have a house full of company, I can't sit here all day waiting."

"Three weeks ago. I saw you, Rebecca, don't try to deny it."

Emma appeared hypnotized by the rushing water, then in a voice so low Rebecca had trouble hearing, she said, "Rebecca, I saw you go into Richard Drummond's house and not come out until the next morning."

Rebecca felt the ground shift beneath her. She said nothing, waiting for Emma to continue.

Emma watched Rebecca's face turn the color of dead ashes in a cold grate. She was delighted with her victory. She said nothing, but waited for Rebecca to speak.

"And when was this?" Rebecca asked. She had decided not to tell Emma they were married. She couldn't help wondering how far Emma would push, now that she thought her back was against the wall. Why did Emma hate her so? Emma was kind to her friends and neighbors, why couldn't she at least be pleasant to her?

"I was right, you have been following me. I knew it." Rebecca tried but failed to make Emma look her in the eye. "You're very bad at spying, Emma, I'd suggest you find another way to occupy your time."

"Don't try to change the subject, you know exactly what I'm talking about. Is that all you have to say about your disgusting behavior!" Emma snorted, "You're nothing, you've always been nothing. My poor papa married you to keep you from becoming the town whore and now you're right back where you started, jumping into everybody's bed. Have you no shame!"

A smile skittered across Rebecca's face and was gone. "It seems to be a case of the kettle calling the pot black, don't you think? How long were you and George married before the baby was born...no, don't answer, it's unimportant and I shouldn't have brought it up."

"Are you going to try and deny it? And stop trying to change the subject."

"You said you saw me. What do you want me to say?" Rebecca said as a look of disgust crossed her face. "Your father said you'd outgrow hating me but he was wrong. Why do you hate me so much? And tell me, Emma, now that you've caught me, as you say, red-handed, just what are you going to do, spread it all over town? You'd better give it a little more thought before you tear down your own world along with mine. You know the old saying about biting off your nose to spite your face." Emma's hands were shaking — whether from fear or hate, Rebecca was unable to tell. "Do you hate me that much?"

Emma's bony knuckles looked ready to break through the skin. She glared at Rebecca, unable to hide her hatred.

"You're not even ashamed of what you've done, you don't care what people think or what you're doing to the rest of the family." The words whipped out of Emma's taut, white lips. "And you're right, I've always hated you."

"I've got to go, I have work to do." Rebecca looked over her shoulder toward the picnic tables.

Emma stood alone at the edge of the river watching Rebecca cross the lawn. She couldn't speak, she was so furious, it certainly hadn't gone the way she'd hoped. Rebecca didn't deny or affirm what she'd said and Rebecca was right, there was nothing she could do with the information that wouldn't tarnish her and her children. There was no way she could let everyone know what a whore Rebecca was, but she'd find a way.

Emma slowly started across the lawn toward the house.

Rebecca sat at the head of the table with Anne on one side and Richard on the other. Emma, sitting next to Anne, picked up her napkin and laid it in her lap. She rubbed her finger the length of the napkin, straightening the creases as Anne, who sat next to her, ran her fingers around the edge of her empty teacup. Anne had a smile on her lips as she waited for Rebecca to make her announcement so she was surprised when Rebecca suddenly turned to her and said, "I need a few things in the kitchen, will you come help me?"

Once inside the house Rebecca pulled Anne into the back hall.

"What's the matter, what happened? I saw you talking to Emma, what's she done now?" Anne, who knew Emma only too well, realized something was wrong. Just the smirk on Emma's face told her that.

"Emma knows about Richard and me, she saw me going into Richard's house."

"So…and what did you say to her?"

"I didn't confirm or deny and I didn't tell her we're married. I was right, she was following me all the time. She'll never change. She's a dangerous woman."

"Rebecca, what difference does it make? You're married, there's nothing she can do and there's no way she can find when or where you were married."

"I'll make sure she never does. It's just that there are times when I'd like to kill her. Here she's been sneaking around, hiding in hotel lobbies and behind luggage carts trying to catch me so she can ruin me. Why can't she be happy with her husband and children and leave me alone?"

"She didn't mention blackmail did she? Emma doesn't have the highest standards, still it's hard to believe she'd stoop to that, but with Emma, who can tell?" Anne grabbed Rebecca's hand. "We can't stay here, we've got to get back. I can't wait to see her face when you announce your marriage."

Roseanna and Emma were deep in conversation when they returned. "We hardly ever get a chance to talk anymore, what have you been doing?" Roseanna set her cake plate on the table and searched for her napkin.

Emma leaned in close and whispered, "I've got so much to tell you, but you've got to promise not to say anything to anybody, at least not for a while."

"Are you alright? You look upset."

Emma whispered in Roseanna's ear. Roseanna said nothing but her face paled as she listened.

Emma's back was to Rebecca so she didn't see Rebecca stand and tap the blade of her knife against her glass. The sharp twang stopped all conversation and heads turned to look at her.

Emma and Roseanna stopped talking as they waited to hear what Rebecca had to say. "Fourth of July is the one day of the year we are all together," Rebecca began,

"It's hard to get together when we're all so busy. Every year we hear about each others' accomplishments and welcome new family members." Rebecca looked down the table at Roseanna and smiled. "This Fourth is special, not only because of birthdays but because I'd like to introduce you to a new family member: my husband, Richard Drummond."

There was a gasp followed by a thunderous clapping of hands.

Emma felt as if she'd been hit in the stomach with a baseball bat. Perspiration broke out on her forehead and upper lip. She patted her face with her napkin. Her face was the color of a snow cloud. Roseanna grabbed Emma's arm. "Are you okay? You look like you're going to be sick."

Emma turned and looked at Roseanna. "I'm okay. Hand me that glass of lemonade, will you?"

"Will you be okay? I want to go and talk to my mother."

"I'm alright, I'll just sit here for a minute."

Roseanna walked to the end of the table. She was unable to get close to her mother as everyone was crowded around, hugging and kissing. She felt an arm across her shoulders and knew without looking who it was. "Aunt Anne, did you know this all the time?"

"Not until a few minutes ago. What's the matter with Emma, her stomach upset?"

"She said it's the heat, but she looks terrible."

"Where's George? He usually comes with her and the girls?"

Before Roseanna could answer Rebecca said, "I hope you weren't too surprised, I wanted to tell you, but Richard thought it better if we waited and told everybody at the same time."

Roseanna threw her arms around her mother's neck. "Momma, I'm delighted. Richard's been a part of the family for years and this just makes it more permanent." She looked at her mother's happy face and couldn't help but delight in her mother's happiness.

Emma walked toward Rebecca. "Congratulations, Rebecca. I hope you'll be very happy." She reached over and gave her an icy kiss on the cheek. Dropping her voice she snarled, "You could have told me before."

Rebecca stepped back and whispered in return. She didn't like standing this close, so close she could feel the warmth of Emma's body. "What, when you were enjoying your little victory so much? Never." Rebecca paused and looked closely at Emma, "Maybe you'd better sit down. You don't look well."

Emma's expression was one of disbelief, as if she'd found herself alone in the middle of the ocean with no oars, life jacket or boat. Emma blotted tears with her napkin, but she couldn't stop them from running down her face.

"You took my father away. You always hated me."

Give Emma a few minutes and she'll be her usual rotten old self, Rebecca thought. "Emma, for heavens' sake, you were a child, why would I hate you?"

"Well, you did and I knew it even then."

Rebecca took a step toward the table. "I think you'd be wise to go now. And don't come back, ever. There's nothing we have to say to each other, now or ever."

Her shoulders hunched, Emma ran across the lawn toward her daughters.

Rebecca turned to find Anne standing behind her. "Doesn't look like Emma's taking your announcement very well. Too bad, it should have happened years ago," Anne said.

Rebecca shook her head. "What's the matter, is Emma sick?" Roseanna was getting ready to remove the tablecloth.

"Sit down, darling." Rebecca patted the place at the end of the bench, "I have something to tell you, about Emma."

"Oh, Emma's already told you!" Roseanna didn't pause for breath. "Didn't you wonder why she and the girls came to the party alone and where George was? But I never thought he'd run off with another woman, did you? You know who she is, she's the one who set up that dance studio on Main street. Did Emma tell you he's been gone a couple of weeks?" Roseanna paused but neither her mother nor Anne said anything. "He told her he was tired of being alone. She was always some place else, like church, or visiting friends, but he said the end came when she started going to Boston two or three times a month. That was too much for him." Roseanna was fighting to hold back her tears. "Poor Emma, what will she do now?"

Rebecca and Anne looked at each other in amazement.

"Emma will always find a way. Don't worry about her." Anne snorted.

Chapter Thirty-three

Kate dropped the letter on the bed. She was reluctant to let her family go, even if only on paper.

It was impossible to imagine her grandmother in love, or her mother, Roseanna, for that matter. Impossible to picture them young, energetic, happy newly-weds. Old people seemed to have always been old. But for the letters she would have missed it all, the deaths, the births, the parties, the romances. A shiver passed through her as she thought how close she'd come to destroying them.

Katie didn't remember Emma, probably never saw her, but she'd never forget her grandmother Rebecca or her Aunt Anne. It wasn't the letters that brought them to life; she knew them, she'd sat in their laps, listened as they read her stories, kissed them goodnight, but the letters turned them into people who loved, cried, hated and laughed long before she'd been born.

The colors in the quilt were as many and varied as those in David's coat. The rose colors had faded to a light shade of pink and the blacks to gray, but others looked as if they'd been sewn on yesterday. Could the yellowish satin come from her grandmother's wedding dress, and the blue one with the tiny flowers from the dress her mother wore the first day she went to school?

Did her mother Roseanna make a quilt as she told Grant she was going to? Could it be packed away some place in her mother's attic?

Katie looked at the quilt folded over the back of the rocker. It had been hung on the line and now smelled as sweet as new mown hay. She opened it and spread it across the bed. Her hand caressed the different colors, passing over her family history. Despite the heat Katie crawled under the quilt and closed her eyes.